国家出版基金项目
NATIONAL PUBLICATION FOUNDATION

Planned by Zhuang Zhixiang   Edited by Pan Wenguo

READINGS OF CHINESE CULTURE SERIES

—— ACADEMICS Ⅱ ——

To Attain Innate Knowledge
– *Records of the Instructions and Reviews* and Yangming's Mindology

Translated by Gong Haiyan

中国经典文化走向世界丛书

学术卷 二

庄智象◎总策划   潘文国◎总主编
龚海燕◎译

上海外语教育出版社
SHANGHAI FOREIGN LANGUAGE EDUCATION PRESS
www.sflep.com

图书在版编目(CIP)数据

中国经典文化走向世界丛书. 学术卷. 二/龚海燕译.
—上海：上海外语教育出版社，2018
ISBN 978-7-5446-5512-5

I. ①中… II. ①龚… III. ①中国文学—综合作品集—英文
IV. ①I211

中国版本图书馆CIP数据核字(2018)第162837号

出版发行：上海外语教育出版社

(上海外国语大学内)　邮编：200083
电　　话：021-65425300（总机）
电子邮箱：bookinfo@sflep.com.cn
网　　址：http://www.sflep.com
责任编辑：李振荣

印　　刷：上海盛通时代印刷有限公司
开　　本：635×965　1/16　印张 10.75　字数 172千字
版　　次：2018 年 11 月第 1 版　2018 年 11 月第 1 次印刷
印　　数：1 100 册

书　　号：ISBN 978-7-5446-5512-5 / B
定　　价：35.00 元

本版图书如有印装质量问题，可向本社调换

质量服务热线：4008-213-263　电子邮箱：editorial@sflep.com

"Cherish one's own beauty, respect other's beauty, and when both beauties are respected and cherished, the world will become one", said Fei Xiaotong, a famous Chinese sociologist at a celebration party in honor of his eightieth birthday about thirty years ago. In a time of growing interest in intercultural communication today, these words sound especially wise and far-sighted. Translation, as one of the most important means for cultural communication, is usually done into one's mother tongue from other languages by native translators. This largely guarantees the quality of translated text, so far as the linguistic readability is concerned. However, this method implies a one-sidedness in correspondence, as only the translator's "respect for other's beauty" is concerned, regardless, though not completely, of how the local people look upon and cherish their own beauty. It should be compensated by translations on the other way, that is, works selected, interpreted, and translated by the local people themselves into languages other than their own. This approach may go directly against the prevalent views in modern translation theories but, in my opinion, is worthy of practicing. It is perhaps an even more effective way to bring about successful communication in cultures, and the beauties of the world can really be shared by the world's people. It is with such understanding that the Shanghai Foreign Languages Education Press is organizing a new series of books, entitled *Readings of Chinese Culture*, to introduce Chinese culture, past and present, to the world, with works selected and translated by the Chinese scholars and translators.

The series will cover a wide range of writings including but not restricted to works of different literary genres. For the first batch, we are glad to provide three books of essays and one book of short stories, all written by authors of the 20th century. They will be continued by a batch of serious academic writings on premodern Chinese classics in philosophy, literature, and historiography, written by influential scholars of our time.

Later, we will offer more books on classical Chinese drama, classical Chinese poetry, etc.

Some of the books in the series have been published before, but they have been revised and rearranged for the new purpose to meet the current needs of broader readers. We are looking forward to hearing comments and suggestions on the series for future improvement.

Pan Wenguo

CONTENTS

INTRODUCTION

Through years of efforts of the authors and translators, the Chinese-English Series of Pre-modern Chinese Classics and Traditional Culture has finally come under publication. The word *pre-modern* here refers to a specific period in Chinese history between *ancient* and *modern*, starting, as I propose, from the Song Dynasty.

The Song Dynasty is a very important period in China which, in a sense, marks the end of the classical China and the beginning of the pre-modern China. Before the Song Dynasty, China had always been a society of aristocrats when all important persons known to us, even the humblest ones like Tao Yuanming or Du Fu, had an aristocratic or noble background, whereas from the Song Dynasty on, common people from grassroots might have a chance to enter the elitist gentry; in fact, certain people from poor families had even become prime ministers or esteemed scholars in the Song Dynasty. The reason is that the imperial examination system which was founded in the Sui and Tang Dynasties was brought into full play in the Song Dynasty and yielded its best effect. "A muddy-footed farmer in the morning, an official in the emperor's court in the evening" became a realizable dream and the social strata became a convective and lively one. At the same time, thanks to the imperial policy which lay more emphasis on culture than on army, education and cultural undertakings were highly encouraged, which made the Song Dynasty the most wealthy and prosperous period in the history of China or even the world. What was described in the famous genre painting of *A Clear Bright Day on the River* by Zhang Zeduan and the famous tune-poem *Watching the Sea Tide* by Liu Yong, or recorded in the memoirs of *The Prosperous Days in Kaifeng* by Meng Yuanlao and *The Past Memories of Hangzhou* by Zhou Mi reflected the thriving and vigorous civil life never found in earlier dynasties, and gave us a direct impression that the Song and the Tang belong to two different epochs with the Song much closer to us. The much talked-about "four great inventions of China", with the exception of *paper*, were achieved in the Song Dynasty and introduced to the West, leading to the great Renaissance in Europe.

Culturally speaking, the Song Dynasty is an epoch of historic importance which creates the future by inheriting the past. This is a time when all the past cultural achievements were inherited and summarized; it is also a time when people made cultural achievements to influence the coming times till today in China as well as in East Asia. It might not be everybody's knowledge that the "traditional China" or "Chinese tradition" we talk about proudly today was not that of the Han, Tang or pre-Qin as we imagine or believe, but was actually created from the Song Dynasty, or reshaped by the Song people in the name of earlier periods. For instance, in the May Fourth Movement in 1919, people raised the banner of "Down with the Kong stash (Confucian doctrines)", but their criticism should actually be targeted at the "Zhu stash", as what they repudiated was not the doctrines of Kong Zi or Meng Zi, but the doctrine of Cheng Yi and Zhu Xi, only disguised as the former. And the Confucianism or neo-Confucianism many people have been advocating since the 1930s till today is actually a resurgence of the Song-Ming Principlism. Using the method of "elaboration instead of creation", Zhu Xi successfully transformed Kong ideology into Zhu ideology, which later became the dominant ideology especially since the Ming Dynasty as it was adopted as the only authorized standard for imperial examinations. The methodology of Zhu Xi is a typical example of the Song scholars, which was adopted by other people in other fields as well. Everyone is familiar with the stories of "two Sima's". The former refers to Sima Qian in the Han Dynasty who created the chronological-biographical style in writing history, thus laying the foundation of the 25 orthodox histories in China, whereas the latter refers to Sima Guang in the Song Dynasty who, by continuing the tradition of *Spring-Autumn Annals* in the ancient time, revived the annalistic style in history writing, thus not only successfully inheriting the achievement of the past 17 *Histories*, but also opening a broader way for later history writing such as the event-focused style and the outline-focused style. Zheng Qiao of the Southern Song Dynasty found another new path by emphasizing the memorandum part of *Historical Records* and *History of the Han Dynasty* and spent his whole life finishing the book *Comprehensive Study of Memorandums,* a vital complement to Sima Guang's book which merely reorganized the biography part of *Histories.* The two books formed another tradition in historical studies, working side by side with the orthodox 25 *Histories* and impacting the historical study till today.

From the above examples we conclude that one cannot really understand China and Chinese tradition without studying the Song Dynasty and its cultural contribution. However, for a very long time in our translation and introduction of Chinese culture to the world, we lay too much emphasis on the pre-Qin part and neglect the Song Dynasty. The pre-Qin classics and philosophical works have had more than scores of translations while important books since the Song Dynasty, save poetry, plays and novels, have drawn little attention and translation. We translated *Confucian Analects* and *Mencius*, but did not know that the "feudal ideology" which had restrained the Chinese nation for centuries did not come directly from them but from the Song-Ming Principlism; we translated *Laoze* and *Zhuangzi* but did not know that what influenced the thoughts of intellectuals after the Song Dynasty was already an amalgam that merged Daoism, Confucianism and Buddhism, with the Chan Buddhism playing a very important role. Realizing this, we planned to do something to fill in the blank so as to draw attention from home and abroad to the introduction of the *pre-modern* cultural literature, of which the present series is the initial step.

The role of the Song Dynasty as a linkage between the ancient and the modern can be seen principally in the several "great" books or anthologies. In the early Northern Song period there already appeared the "four great works" of *Taiping Imperial Encyclopedia, Referential Records from Imperial Archives, Taiping Miscellany* and *Choice Blossoms of Literature*, three out of the four containing 1,000 volumes. These were doubtlessly the representative establishments of the Song culture. The *Kaibao Tripitaka* laid the foundation for the Buddhist pitaka compilation. The *Enlarged Rhyming Dictionary*, the

Collected Rhyming Dictionary, the *Enlarged Sinographic Dictionary* and the *Classified Sinographic Dictionary* marked new achievements in dictionary compilation. The *History as a Mirror for Governance* opened up a new path for historiography. The *Comprehensive Study of Memorandums* served as an important continuation in the formation of the ten *Comprehensives.* Hong Mai's *Miscellaneous Notes from the Tolerance Study,* Shen Kuo's *Pen Talk in the Dreamed Creek Garden* and Wang Yinglin's *Record of Observances from Arduous Studies* marked the beginning of pre-modern academic research. Although the *Complete Works of Zhu Xi* was compiled just recently, most of the works contained therein were already popular in the late Song Dynasty. Among them, the *Collected Annotations to the Four Books,* the *Close Reflections,* and the *Classified Analects of Zhu Xi* even became the most important textbooks of Principlism during the 700 years from the late Song Dynasty to the beginning of the 20th century. And from Zhu Xi one would naturally relate to Wang Yangming whose Mindology had played no less important role since the mid-Ming Dynasty. Thus we decided to introduce the pre-modern classics and their influence to Chinese culture by way of introducing some "great books" and their developments. In the present series we have chosen six books. They are respectively, the *Complete Works of Zhu Xi,* the *Records of Instructions and Reviews,* the *History as a Mirror for Governance,* the *Choice Blossoms of Literature,* the *Taiping Miscellany,* and the *Buddhist Tripitaka.* And we invited established experts in relevant areas to write concise, introductory books in the manner of "big heads preparing small pamphlets", before asking English experts with Chinese study background to translate them into English. Specifically, the authors and translators of the six books are:

> *Complete Works of Zhu Xi and Its Inheritance,* written by Fu Huisheng, annotated & translated by Pan Wenguo
>
> *To Attain Innate Knowledge — Records of the Instructions and Reviews and Yangming's Mindology,* written by Yang Guorong, translated by Gong Haiyan
>
> *History as a Mirror for Governance and Chinese Historiography,*

written by Zhuang Huiming, translated by Zhang Chunbai

Choice Blossoms of Literature and the Trends of Pre-modern Poetry and Prose, written by Chen Yinchi, translated by Zhang Deshao

The Buddhist Triptaka in Chinese and Its Cultural Concern, written by Li Xiangping, translated by Fu Huisheng

You may find in the list not a few names very familiar to the academic circles. For example, Professor Yang Guorong is the Changjiang Scholar of the State Ministry of Education and dean of the School of Humanities and Social Sciences of East China Normal University (ECNU), Professor Zhuang Huiming is the ex-vice-president of ECNU and dean of Meng Xiancheng Academy, Professor Chen Yinchi is head of the Department of Chinese Language and Literature of Fudan University and "Talent of the New Century" assigned by the State Ministry of Education, Professor Chen Dakang is the former head of the Department of Chinese Language and Literature, former head of the ECNU Library as well as member of the Discipline Appraisal Group of the Degree Committee of the State Council, Professor Li Xiangping is head of the Department of Sociology of ECNU and vice-chairman of Shanghai Society for Religious Studies, Professor Zhang Chunbai is the former dean of the School of Foreign Languages of ECNU and member of the Guidance Committee for Teaching Foreign Languages of the State Ministry of Education, as well as the vice chairman of the Shanghai Society of Foreign Languages, Professor Fu Huisheng is head of the Department of International Chinese Studies of ECNU and standing council member of China Association for Comparative Studies between English and Chinese, so on and so forth. Their participation is an important guarantee of the success of the present series. Here I would like to express my personal gratitude to these eminent scholars!

The plan for this series actually started a dozen of years ago and many authors handed their manuscripts rather early. It's mainly my delay and the difficulty in translation that had kept the process so long. Now, with the efforts of all the authors and translators, this series is finally under publication. Special thanks must go to Professor Fu Huisheng who personally took up the writing of one book and the translation of another two books. Besides, he has helped me to read over most of the manuscripts of translations. Without his persistence the series would not be successful.

Finally, I would like to extend my thanks to Shanghai Foreign Language Education Press and its president and editor-in-chief, Professor Zhuang Zhixiang, who has been unswervingly in support of the country's foreign languages teaching cause, and who, in recent years, has shown special concern for promoting the traditional Chinese culture to the world. Without their support, this seemingly unpopular title would not have an opportunity to go to the public.

Pan Wenguo

Shanghai

June 28, 2016

Chapter One

Evolution of the Principlism: Historical Prerequisite for the Formation of Mindology

During the Song and Ming Dynasties, a series of classical philosophical works were gradually published along with the development of the Principlism, and *Records of the Instructions and Reviews* by Wang Yangming[①] was a prominent one. Although not in great length, it is an important book of Wang Yangming's Mindology, which exerted a far-reaching influence on the Chinese intellectual and cultural history after the middle of the Ming Dynasty. When we review the Chinese intellectual history in about four hundred years, we always have to trace back to this philosophical classic that epitomizes Wang Yangming's Mindology.

As a ramification of the Principlism, the formation of Wang Yangming's Mindology relied on the development of the Principlism as its prerequisite. Therefore, in order to have a good command of the meanings of the Mindology, we must first make a brief examination of the course of the evolution of the Principlism and the relevant problems involved.

1. Nature is Principle, and Others: Intensification of Metaphysical Noumenon

The relation between Mind and Nature is an important issue for

---

① Wang Yangming (1472 – 1529), a celebrated philosopher, educator, calligrapher, and government official of the Ming Dynasty. He is commonly regarded as the most important Neo-Confucian thinker after Zhu Xi.

analysis in the Principlism. It is because of the focal concern on Mind and Nature that the Principlism is often called the Study of Mind and Nature. The first scholars who made the systematic examination of the relation between Mind and Nature are two Cheng brothers (Cheng Hao[1] and Cheng Yi[2]) and Zhu Xi[3].

In Chengs-Zhu's view, Mind referred to general spiritual activity and spiritual phenomena, and was connected with man's sensitive existence. Two Chengs said: "Every man is born with Nature, and the master of body is Mind." (*The Posthumous Writings of Two Chengs*, vol.18) Man, being opposite to body, is emphasized for the universal essence as human beings, whereas body is primarily connected with the sensible life of an individual. The master of body implies not only the restraint of intelligent apperception of Mind over body, but also the infiltration of sensitive existence into Mind.

Mind as the unity of intelligent apperception and sensitive existence often manifests an original state (original suchness). From original state to oughtness (a should-be state), there is an involvement of the relations between Mind and Principle, and Mind and Nature. Zhu Xi held that Mind and Principle were not separable from each other: "Mind and Principle are in unity." (*Ibid.*) The unity of Principle and Mind does not mean they are identical to each other or blended into oneness. It unfolds concretely an existence of Principle in Mind: "Mind embodies all Principles, and all Principles are embodied in one Mind." (*Ibid.* vol.9) Embodiment of Principle in Mind means that Principle is in and dominates Mind. Principle in Mind is also Nature: "Principle in Mind of man is Nature." (*Categorized Quotations from Zhuzi*, vol.98). In Chengs-Zhu's view, the relation between Nature and Principle was quite different

---

[1] Cheng Hao (1032 – 1085), a philosopher of the Northern Song Dynasty. He and his younger brother Cheng Yi were among the pioneers of the Song Dynasty Neo-Confucianism.
[2] Cheng Yi (1033 – 1107), a philosopher of the Northern Song Dynasty. He lived and taught in Luoyang, and gave lectures to the emperor on Confucianism.
[3] Zhu Xi (1130 – 1200), a prominent philosopher, writer and government official of the Southern Song Dynasty. He was the leading figure of the School of Principlism and the most influential rationalist Neo-Confucian in China. He made contributions to Chinese philosophy by assigning special significance to the Four Books.

from the relation between Mind and Principle. Nature as Principle in Mind shares the identity with Principle. It is in this sense that Chengs-Zhu repeatedly emphasized: "Nature is Principle. It is called Nature in Mind, and Principle in Thing." (*Ibid.*) Mind and Principle often manifest a relation of inclusion, as indicated in "All Principles exist in Mind", or "Mind embodies all Principles". This relation mainly focuses on the two mutually related aspects: Mind holds Principle as its substance, and Principle is the master of Mind. Hence, according to Chengs-Zhu's view, in discussion of Nature, it could certainly be said that Nature was Principle (the word "was" has the meaning of "oneness"); but in talking about Mind, it could not be said in the same sense that Mind was Principle.

In elucidation of the connotations of Mind and Nature respectively, Chengs-Zhu at the same time defined their relation. Zhu Xi once compared the Extreme Ultimate (*Taiji*) and *yin-yang* to Nature and Mind: "Nature is like the Extreme Ultimate, and Mind *yin-yang*." (*Categorized Quotations from Zhuzi*, vol. 5) The Extreme Ultimate was often regarded in the works of Chengs-Zhu as the highest form of Principle, and *yin-yang* as *qi* (vital energy); while in the theory of the Way of Heaven, Principle determined *qi*, in the relation between Mind and Nature, Nature determined Mind. The above relation between Mind and Nature was usually much briefly generalized as that "Mind holds Nature as its noumenon." (*Ibid.*) Thus it can be seen that in the domain of Mind and Nature, Chengs-Zhu focused their attention on establishing the supremacy of human nature.

Starting from the prerequisite of Nature as noumenon, Zhu Xi criticized "the explication of Nature with Mind". (*Ibid.* vol.4) Explication of Nature with Mind implies the restoration of Nature to Mind, or the definition of Nature with Mind. Contrary to this, Chengs-Zhu preferred to transform Mind into Nature. This point is easily perceived in the above analysis, and can be further seen in the theory of Mind of Man and Mind of the Way. Mind of Man is mainly associated with sensitive existence (shape of the body), whereas Mind of the Way originates from the universal Principle and is therefore pure out of purity. With regard to Principle as substance, Mind of the Way and Nature are inseparably connected. In fact,

Zhu Xi also affirmed this point: "Nature, therefore, is Mind of the Way." (*Ibid*. vol.61) In Chengs-Zhu's view, the rational relation between Mind of Man and Mind of the Way should be that Mind of Man was in submission to Mind of the Way, and dominance of Mind of the Way implies that Mind of Man should be transformed to Mind of the Way: "With Mind of the Way in dominance, Mind of Man is then transformed into the Mind of the Way." (Reply to Huang Zigeng, *Collected Writings of Master Zhu*, vol.51) In terms of their internal logic, transformation of Mind of Man into Mind of the Way, and transformation of Mind into Nature are the two mutually connected aspects, and both direct to the same goal: purification of perceptual domain with noumenon of Principle-Nature.

The above tendency was further manifested in Chengs-Zhu's theory of Nature and Feeling. Feeling as an aspect of Mind belongs to Mind in a broad sense, and is on the level of perceptual experience. The concrete unfoldment of the relation between Mind and Nature is thus logically involved with the relation between Nature and Feeling. Cheng Yi in his essay "On What Yan Yuan Liked to Learn" put forward the two Principles as to the relation between nature and feeling, i.e., "temper Feeling with Nature" and "temper Nature with Feeling". "Temper Feeling with Nature", first put forward by Wang Bi[1] in his Annotation of the Qian Hexagram of *The Zhou Book of Change*, basically means the dominance of Nature over Feeling and the transformation of Feeling into Nature, while "temper Nature with Feeling" implies the restraint of Nature with Feeling. Cheng Yi absorbed and elucidated Wang Bi's theory of "temper Feeling with Nature", and thus rejected "temper Nature with Feeling". This principle of the relation between Feeling and Nature was repeatedly affirmed later by Zhu Xi. In the same way as transforming Mind of Man into Mind of the Way, "temper Feeling with Nature" reflected the generalized tendency of the essence of Principlist nature: "temper Feeling with Nature" in essence means the rationalization of Feeling. In this process, Feeling of Man in connection with perceptual

---

[1] Wang Bi (226 – 249), a philosopher whose most important works are commentaries on Lao Zi's *Dao De Jing* and *The Zhou Book of Change*.

existence began to lose its relatively independent quality: Only after it was assimilated into the noumenon of the universal Principle could it exist in subjective consciousness. Therefore, it is not difficult to see that Nature as noumenon of Mind is here manifested as the assimilation of emotional experience into Principlist essence.

Chengs-Zhu developed their theories of Mind and Nature with Nature as Principle, Nature as noumenon of Mind, transformation of Mind into Nature, "temper Feeling with Nature", etc., and the internal theme was to construct the position of Nature as noumenon. When Chengs-Zhu held Principle as substance of Mind, and correspondingly Nature as noumenon of Mind, Mind had already begun to be transformed equally to Nature, while through the courses of transformation of Mind of Man into Mind of the Way, "temper Feeling with Nature", etc., the generalized transformation of Mind into Nature obtained its more concrete substance. In Chengs-Zhu's theory, the concrete substance of Nature was manifested as a criterion of oughtness: "Nature is what Man receives from Heaven, and its noumenon is no more than the principles of benevolence, righteousness, propriety and wisdom." (*Questions on Meng Zi* in *Questions on the Four Books*, vol. 14) Here, benevolence, righteousness, propriety and wisdom are the criteria of oughtness, and they in essence belong to the category of the norm of Principlism. As the internalization of the criteria of oughtness, Nature saliently demonstrates the essence of universal Principlism. Such repeated promotion and intensification of Nature-Principle lead to the logic conclusion of establishing the transcendental noumenon of Principlism. In theory, Principlism is one of the essences that differentiate Man from other existences (for instance, animals). Chengs-Zhu emphasized that Nature was Principle, and stressed the distinction of Man from other existences (for instance, fowls and beasts) in the aspect of Principlism. However, excessive emphasis on noumenon of Principlism can often result in the understanding of Man himself as an abstract existence. When Zhu Xi demanded catharsis of Mind of Man with Mind of the Way, he, more or less, ignored the rich definitions of Man in reality and regarded him one-sidedly as an incarnation of Principlism. It is very difficult to put into practice the multiple dimensional development of Man from this standpoint, for the priority of Principlism has the tendency of restraining the attention on the sensitive existence and the dimensions of feeling, will, and intuition. It was right from here that Chengs-Zhu oriented their theory toward essentialism.

The above thinking about the relation between Mind and Nature was also reflected in the outlook of the external world. Zhou Dunyi[1], the founder of Principlism, once drew a diagram of the Extreme Ultimate (*Taiji*) as a basic pattern of evolution of the universe and all things of creation. In *An Explanation of the Extreme Ultimate Diagram*, Zhou Dunyi outlined briefly the pattern of the universe as follows: the Ultimate of Nothingness (*Wuji*) or the shapeless Extreme Ultimate was the supreme Principle of existence of all things of creation, and this ultimate Principle at the same time constituted the origin of the universe. The Ultimate of Nothingness and the Ultimate of Extremity generated the *qi* of *yin-yang*, and the *qi* of *yin-yang* again split into the five phases of metal, wood, water, fire and earth. Further formed from this stage were the alternating four seasons of spring, summer, autumn and winter, until all the things of creation were produced between Heaven and Earth. It can be seen in Zhou's description that the observation of existence and cosmology were inextricably entangled with each other.

The above view of Zhou Dunyi was also reflected in Zhu Xi's theory. Like Zhou, Zhu Xi also understood the Ultimate of Nothingness (the Ultimate of Extremity) as the ultimate existence (noumenon), and regarded this noumenon as the original source of the *qi* of *yin-yang*. In Zhu Xi's view, when traced back from experiential phenomena (all concrete things of creation), all of them originated from the five phases, the five phases were produced from the *qi* of *yin-yang*, and the *qi* of *yin-yang* was rooted in the Extreme Ultimate; therefore, the Extreme Ultimate was the ultimate origin of all things of creation. In a deduction that started from the

---

[1] Zhou Dunyi (1017 – 1073), a philosopher and cosmologist of the Northern Song Dynasty. He is credited as the first philosopher to popularize the concept of the *taiji*.

ultimate existence downward, the Extreme Ultimate again was discretely seen in experiential phenomena. "Root" and "branches" in their original meanings belong to the category of ontology, but in Zhu Xi's theory, they were again connected with the course of cosmological generation: all things of creation were regarded as "branches", and the Extreme Ultimate the "root". Such kind of questions of ontology as noumenon and phenomena, existence and source, were mixed with the questions of cosmological origination, evolution, constitution, etc. Bearing much similarity with Zhou Dunyi's thought, Zhu Xi's observation of existence had obviously the implication of speculative construction.

Of course, in comparison with Zhou Dunyi's theory, Zhu Xi's theory of existence had its own characteristics. Instead of maintaining the pattern of cosmological generation like Zhou Dunyi, Zhu Xi was unsatisfied with the mere provision of a cosmological description of the universe, and attempted to further elucidate existence in regard to the relation between matter and form. In Zhu Xi's view, the universe was an orderly structure, in which Principle and qi each had its own fixed position: "Between Heaven and Earth, there are Principle and qi. Principle is the metaphysical Way, the origin of all things of creation; qi is the physical vessel, the concrete matter of all things of creation. Therefore, the creation of Man and all other things must possess this Principle, and then receive their own Nature; they must possess this qi, and then have their forms." (Reply to Huang Daofu, *Collected Writings of Master Zhu*, vol. 58) In the course of formation of all things, the function of Principle was similar to the formal cause, and that of qi was close to the material cause. Principle as the basis of all things of creation (the metaphysical Way) constitutes the essence of a thing as a thing, and qi then gives its concrete outer form of a thing. Principle and qi (the Way and the vessel) have their own functions respectively, and cannot overstep each other's boundary.

Principle and qi as noumenon and concrete existence of all things of creation, though their functions are different, are dependent on and inseparable from each other as to concrete objects (things). If there is only qi without Principle, then all things of creation lack the internal bases; if there is Principle without *qi*, it is difficult for all things of creation to obtain their materiality. Broadly speaking, it can also be said that Principle and *qi* per se are inseparable: "In the universe, there does not exist *qi* without Principle, neither is there Principle without *qi*." (*Categorized Quotations from Zhuzi*, vol. 1) This mutual relation between Principle and *qi* is primarily reflected as a logic relation: logically speaking, since Principle and *qi* are the two indispensible conditions for all concrete things of creation, when Principle is mentioned, *qi* is embodied in it; at the same time, when *qi* is mentioned, Principle is also embraced in it.

It can be seen from the above that Zhu Xi's observation of existence was roughly expressed in two dimensions: cosmological construction and logic deduction. The former emphasized the exposition of existence from the course of generation and evolution of the universe, and the latter defined existence largely in the logical relation between Principle and *qi*. Although the two dimensions had different focuses, they had a common tendency, i.e. the study of existence outside man's cognitive activity (knowing) and practical activity (acting). This approach of studying the heavenly way as it was had in fact restricted Zhu Xi from getting away from the speculative orientation. In theory, the existence beyond the domain of man's knowledge and practice can be attributed to the original domain. As to this existence, we cannot offer any more explanation except saying that it is being-in-itself or an original existence, as being-in-itself or an original existence is always in opposition to man's knowledge and practice. If the emphasis is only directed at the original domain beyond the course of knowledge and practice, and an attempt is made to expound existence from this point, then surely speculative construction cannot be avoided. In Zhu Xi's "cosmologically speaking" and "logically speaking", it is not difficult for us to see this point.

The transcendental approach in the study of existence also caused the insurmountable theoretical difficulty embedded in Zhu Xi's philosophy. As related above, Zhu Xi inherited Zhou Dunyi's theory and regarded the Extreme Ultimate as the ultimate noumenon ("the root of all things of creation"). As the root of all things of creation, the Extreme Ultimate existed before and transcended all things of creation; therefore, it is difficult for this theory to avoid dualization of the universe. Zhu Xi separated repeatedly the Extreme Ultimate, the root of all things of creation, from concrete objects, i.e. the Extreme Ultimate transcended any specific time and space, and it did not exist in any concrete time and space. It is this attribute of transcendence that made the Extreme Ultimate noumenon of all things of creation; once it was mixed with concrete things into one, then the Extreme Ultimate would not be the noumenon of the root of all things of creation. Here, the Extreme Ultimate as the root of all things of creation, and the specific objects were in two separate orders: the former (the Extreme Ultimate) belonged to the metaphysical domain of noumenon, and the latter (objects) the physical domain of phenomena. The former was "a clean and spatial world, without shape or trace," (*Categorized Quotations from Zhuzi*, vol.1) and the latter had shape and trace, and existed in specific time and space. The speculative course from the Extreme Ultimate to *qi* of *yin* and *yang*, five phases, to all things of creation, only provided a cosmological pattern of generation, and had not really solved the problem of opposition between the metaphysical and physical domains. Therefore, it always remained an insurmountable theoretical difficulty for Zhu Xi to unify the dual worlds.

Such is the case for cosmological construction. Similarly, in the logical study of the relation between Principle and *qi*, the problem itself was there from the start. According to the logical relation between Principle and *qi*, if there exists Principle, there is *qi*; if there is *qi*, then Principle is embodied in it. There does not exist a sequence between Principle and *qi*. However, in Zhu Xi's philosophy, he started with the prerequisite of transcendence, and usually alternated between "cosmologically speaking" and "logically speaking", while the logical coexistence of Principle and *qi*, and the generative relation of Principle and *qi* were often entangled with each other. Principle gave birth to *qi* — that was a generative relation; when there was *qi*, Principle was embodied in it — that was a logic relation. What the two refer to is fundamentally different, but Zhu Xi combined them in one. In correspondence to it was the infinite wavering between the two contradictory themes, "There is no sequence between Principle and *qi*" and "There is a sequence between Principle and *qi*": "There is fundamentally no such a question of sequence between Principle and *qi*. However, if it is a demand for deduction from the origin, then we have to say there is Principle at first." (*Ibid.*) There was no sequence in the logical relation, and there was a sequence in generative relation: they constituted a weird speculative loop. It is always difficult to get out of this weird speculative loop along the approach of transcendence.

In correspondence to the promotion of noumenon of Nature in the distinction between Mind and Nature, and the emphasis on the dominance of the Extreme Ultimate over all things of creation in ontology, the Principlism of the Chengs-Zhu school paid more attention to the restraint of the Heavenly Principle on human behavior in the moral practice. The Heavenly Principle not only had the ontological meaning, but also was the universal norm in the domain of ethics. In Chengs-Zhu's view, the Principle in the latter's sense constituted the possible condition for moral conduct: moral practice meant understanding the universal Principle first, and then practicing in observance of it. As the universal norm, the Principle had the attribute of transcendence. In exposition of the norm of "benevolence", Zhu Xi specifically pointed out, "Benevolence is the have-to-do Principle that heaven ordains me." (*Questions on the Analects of Confucius*, vol.1) "Mandate" is an external order of the Heavenly Principle to a subject; herein "I" as a conductor and the Heavenly Principle as the universal norm constitute the two opposite polarities, while "my" conduct demonstrates conscious submission to the universal norm.

As the mandate of heaven, the norm not only has been a kind of oughtness, but at the same time possesses the attribute of necessity: the "have-to-do" already implies "must-be-so". In fact, Zhu Xi indeed attempted to combine oughtness with necessity. It is not difficult to see the intention from the following remark: "The relations between monarch and subject, father and son, husband and wife, old and young, and between friends are constant virtues; they are all criteria of oughtness that must be adhered to regardless of oneself, for they are Principles." (Zhu Xi: *Questions on the Great Learning*, vol.2) The adherence to the criteria regardless of oneself represents a tendency of necessity: understanding the criteria of oughtness as principles that must be adhered to regardless of oneself means regarding oughtness as necessity. Heavenly Principle as the external mandate that must be adhered to regardless of oneself at the same time assumes some obligatory attribute: It is not out of self choice to follow Heavenly Principle, but a have-to-do thing, as indicated in "Filial piety and fraternal love are the mandate of heaven to me as have-to-do things." (*Ibid*. vol.1) This conduct out of the heavenly mandate obviously has the characteristic of the restraint from an external order.

Of course, besides the external opposition between the heavenly mandate and oneself, Zhu Xi also discussed from a different aspect the relation between the criterion of oughtness and self. In his theory of Mind of the Way and Mind of Man, we can see this point. In terms of form, Mind of the Way as the Principlist definition in subject had already obtained certain internal form, and its restraint on Mind of Man and his conduct correspondingly seemed to have the meaning of "self-determination" of subject. However, it is not difficult to see with some further study that the Mind of the Way Zhu Xi meant was not the real true self. As the internalization of the Heavenly Principle, it possessed more of the attribute of transcendence of individual: the distinction between Mind of the Way and Mind of Man at the same time also demonstrated the opposition between transcendental Principle and individual existence. Zhu Xi demanded that Mind of Man must absolutely submit itself to Mind of the Way, which meant that the internalized universal Principle dominated over the choice of man's conduct. Although there was a distinction between the internal and external ways in the function of norms, there seemed to be no difference between the two in affirmation of the point that the conduct of man should unconditionally follow the universal norms.

Chengs-Zhu demanded that the conduct of man abide by universal Principlist norms, and no doubt they noticed that moral conduct should be self-conscious. This view avoided the confusion of moral practice with spontaneous impulsion or sensitive activity, and also stressed in one aspect moral loftiness and dignity. However, the norms as general laws and decrees have the transcendental attribute. The emphasis on general norms regulating oneself leads to the unavoidable heteronomy of moral practice (passive observance of the external orders), and is likely to cause unwillingness in action, making it difficult to achieve a natural inclination to goodness. As a matter of fact, in the form of heavenly mandate or Mind of the Way, moral norms often become compulsory laws and decrees, thus it is unavoidable to have a sense of submission to heteronymous rules and laws in abidance by the norms. The opposition between the external heavenly Principle and the subject constitutes another theoretical problem within Chengs-Zhu's Principlism.

2.   Lu Jiuyuan①: Tension between Mind and Principle

Almost at the same time when Zhu Xi was perfecting the theory of the two Chengs' school, Lu Jiuyuan also formed his system of Mindology. Although Lu was not outside the trend of the Principlism, he had serious disagreement with Zhu Xi on many issues. They had repeated debates through letters over the relations between Principle and *qi*, etc.

Lu Jiuyuan once wrote to Zhu Xi, criticizing the latter's views on the relation between Principle and *qi*. He held that Zhu Xi only regarded *qi* of *yin-yang* as form and vessel, and excluded it from the Way, which meant that Zhu did not understand the distinction between the Way and vessel. This can be regarded as his challenge to Zhu Xi's affirmation of Principle (the Way) as transcendental substance. In Lu Jiuyuan's view, the Way and vessel could not be separated, and the Way did not exist outside of any concrete thing: "There is not a thing outside the Way, and there is not the Way outside a thing." There is no doubt that this view denied Zhu Xi's speculative tendency of dualization of the universe. In ethics and values, Lu Jiuyuan was also quite dissatisfied with the opposition between Heavenly Principle and human desire: "The argument about the relation between

---

① Lu Jiuyuan (1139 – 1192), a philosopher and Confucian scholar of the Southern Song Dynasty. He was a contemporary and the academic rival of Zhu Xi.

Heavenly Principle and human desire is certainly not perfect remark itself. If Heaven is Heaven, Man is Man, then Heaven and Man are different." (*Collected Writings of Lu Jiuyuan*, Zhonghua Book Company, 1980, 395) Here, it is certain that he did not affirm the legitimacy of human desire, but objected to the opposition between Heavenly Principle and Man as subject. Behind the repudiation of the view that "Heaven is Heaven, Man is Man" is the criticism of Zhu Xi's theory of opposition between external Heavenly Principle and individual existence.

Although he noticed some inherent problems in Zhu Xi's philosophy, Lu Jiuyuan had his own problems in his system. As for the relation between Mind and Nature, in contrast with Chengs-Zhu's proposition that "Nature is Principle", Lu Jiuyuan put forth the proposition that "Mind is Principle". When expounding this theory, he, on the one hand, repeatedly explained Mind as an individual Mind, demanded "the greatest satisfaction of my Mind", and emphasized that this Mind fully followed "my own will": "As a man controls his ears, if he wants to listen, he just listens; if he does not want to listen, he will not listen. It is the same with his eyes. Why can Mind alone not be in my control?" (*Ibid.* 439) Here Mind seems to be categorized into the same series of sensory organs of ears, eyes, etc., and is mainly subjected to individual will. This Mind completely determined by individual will (by self Mind) in fact represents a kind of individual will, from which the universal norms of Principle, Nature, etc. have been extracted.

On the other hand, Lu Jiuyuan repeatedly stressed the universal quality of Mind: "By 'Mind', we mean there only exists a sole Mind. My Mind, my friend's Mind, or Mind of sages and superior men for over a hundred or a thousand years in the past, and again the Mind of another sage or superior man in the next hundred or a thousand years — these are all the same." (*Ibid.* 444) "When a sage comes from the east sea, his Mind is the same, and the Principle is the same; when a sage comes from the west sea, his Mind is the same, and the Principle is the same; when sages come from the south and north seas, their Minds are the same, and the Principles are the same." (*Ibid.* 388) Hundreds or thousands of years ago, and hundreds or thousands of years in the future are mainly in terms of time, and east sea, west sea and so on in terms of space; that is to say, whenever and wherever there is the existence of man, there is the universal Mind which coincides with the universal Principle, while the qualities of different individuals are relatively nullified.

Lu Jiuyuan's views are obviously difficult to be self-compatible in theory: when he listed Mind together with sensory organs such as ears, eyes, etc., and called it "my Mind", Mind seems to be identical with specific sensory existences; when Mind was defined as eternity in time (no distinction between before and after, between past and present), and limitless existence in space (no differences between east and west, between south and north), it again obtained a transcendental quality. The above dual definition on Mind-Body leaves an internal tension in Lu Jiuyuan's Mindology that is difficult to eliminate.

In the works of Lu Jiuyuan's disciples, the individualistic aspect of Mindology seemed to have received more attention. For instance, Yang Jian, one of Lu's disciples, started from the emphasis on individuality and elaborated "I as the first original Principle". "Heaven and earth are my heaven and earth; changes, my changes." "In heaven there are celestial phenomena; on earth there are patterns and forms; they are all my works." (*Posthumous Writings of Cihu*, vol.7) Here Lu Jiuyuan's Mindology had actually begun to develop towards solipsism.

3. Wavering between the Theories of Zhu Xi and Lu Jiuyuan

The Principlism underwent further evolution from the end of the Southern Song Dynasty to the beginning of the Ming Dynasty. Some principlists tried to readjust Chengs-Zhu's prejudice, but failed to walk out of Chengs-Zhu's line of thinking; some other Principlists focused on promotion of Lu Jiuyuan's Mindology, but often failed to avoid making the same mistakes.

The opposition between the external Heavenly Principle and the subject remained an unsolved problem for Chengs-Zhu's philosophy. How could the unity of the two be achieved? Zhu Xi's disciple Zhen Dexiu[1] made a serious study in this aspect. In Zhen Dexiu's view, Principle as the universal original Principle was not outside of any concrete thing: it existed in things; as Man himself was also a "thing", Principle was also not outside of Man. Here, Principle underwent the transformation from external obligatory norm into internalized criterion of the subject. In Zhen Dexiu's view, this internalized norm of the subject had the characteristic of perfect harmony with the subject. When subject and norm were separated from each other, i.e. the Way was the Way and I was I, conduct often had compulsory and heteronymous characteristics. Only when the universal Way was internalized in the subject could this sense of compulsion be eliminated to realize "happiness of the sage and the superior man".

Xu Heng[2], another follower of Zhu Xi, also demonstrated similar speculative tendency as Zhen Dexiu. Xu Heng first made a distinction between "why-so" and "should-be": "Why-so is fate, and should-be is righteousness." (*Academic Cases of the Confucian Scholars in the Song and Yuan Dynasties*, vol.90) "Fate" is here manifested as a kind of necessity, and "righteousness" a kind of obligation. "Why-so" and "should-be" were at first the dual definition of Principle by Zhu Xi. In Zhu Xi's theory, the two were completely overlapping: why-so was should-be. In departure from Zhu Xi's view, Xu Heng thought the two could not be completely identical. On one hand, why-so as the external necessity was not subjected to man's will, i.e. "not within self control"; on the other hand, the subject should behave at his own will, i.e. "of his own accord". It was based on this view that Xu Heng maintained that moral education should stress cultivation and inspiration of innate knowledge of the subject, and opposed the mandatory restraint of Man with Heavenly Principle.

Of course, in demanding the connection between Heavenly Principle and the subject, Zhen Dexiu and Xu Heng did not deny the universal

---

[1] Zhen Dexiu (1178 – 1235), a philosopher and government official of the Southern Song Dynasty. His influence at the imperial court made Neo-Confucianism the dominant philosophy of his time.

[2] Xu Heng (1209 – 1281), an educator and Confucian scholar of the Jin-Yuan period. He was the first leader of the National Academy of the Yuan Dynasty.

restraint of Heavenly Principle. Ever since Zhou Dunyi, Principlists had been taking delight in talking about "Kong-Yan's happiness". Although Kong Zi (Confucius) and Yan Hui (one of Confucius's disciples) lived in a crude house in a small lane with simple diet, they maintained an optimistic attitude in life. What they pursued was a spiritual happiness beyond sensual desires. In Zhen Dexiu's view, true realization of this conception demanded that one "swim in Heavenly Principle with ease", i.e. maintain self-restraint consciously with Heavenly Principle. Zhen Dexiu believed that self-conscious submission to Heavenly Principle was the prerequisite for attainment of the Kong-Yan's happiness, and emphasized the guideline of Principlism. Similarly, Xu Heng upheld the supremacy of Heavenly Principle, and thought that "One Principle can command all things of creation." (*Posthumous Writings of Luzhai*, vol.2) That is a demand of directing all Man's conduct with Heavenly Principle. In regard to this, both Zhen Dexiu and Xu Heng did not surpass Zhu Xi's line of thinking that Principle was the first (original) driving force.

In opposition to the elucidation of Zhen Dexiu and Xu Heng on Zhu Xi's thought, some Principlists in the Yuan Dynasty began to shift their attention to Lu Jiuyuan's philosophy. In this aspect, Wu Cheng and Zheng Yu were, to a certain extent, the representatives. In the relation between Mind and the Way, Wu Cheng held that the Way existed in Mind, and there was not the Way outside Mind: "The Way as the Way exists only in Mind. How can it be possible to find the Way outside Mind?" (*Academic Cases of the Confucian Scholars in the Song and Yuan Dynasties*, vol.92) Not only did the Way exist inside Mind, but also all things of creation under heaven existed in Mind. Starting from the view that all things of creation were not outside Mind, Wu Cheng opposed the belief that the Way should be attributed to a substance that transcended all concrete things. In his view, although there was the metaphysical and physical distinction between the universal Way and concrete things, the two were not separated from each other. In contrast with the Chengs-Zhu's Principlism that regarded the metaphysical Way and physical things as a dual world, Wu Cheng undoubtedly paid more attention to the unity of the two. However, because of affirmation of the existence of the Way and things in Mind, Wu Cheng again overstressed the importance of self, and believed that Self-Mind was at the same time the master of all things of creation, and thus demonstrated certain inclination of solipsism.

At the beginning of the Ming Dynasty, the development of Principlism still wavered between the theoretic patterns of Zhu Xi and Lu Jiuyuan. Relatively speaking, the Principlists in the early Ming Dynasty stressed the "exposition of Zhu Xi's theory", i.e. explication and elucidation of Zhu Xi's thought. As to the relation between Heavenly Principle and the subject, Xue Xuan, a famous Principlist at the beginning of the Ming Dynasty, believed that Principle and the Way were ubiquitous: from tangible things to intangible social ethical relations, they were all embedded with Principle and the Way. This universality of Principle and the Way determined that Man could not walk out of the scope Heavenly Principle functioned in. It is starting from this prerequisite that Xue Xuan emphasized that all activities of Man, no matter big or small, should be included in Heavenly Principle. In the vast net of Principle and the Way, independency of Man seemed to be overshadowed completely in the dominance of Heavenly Principle. This view obviously fails to transcend the dual opposition between Principle and Man.

Soon after Xue Xuan, Hu Juren, another Principlist in the first half of the Ming Dynasty, also inherited Chengs-Zhu's view. In the relation between Principle and *qi*, Hu Juren held that there was a sequence between them: Principle came first and then there was *qi*. As the determiner of qi, Principle possessed the attribute of transcending all things of creation. Accordingly, in the relation between Heavenly Principle and self, Hu Juren mentioned that Mind of Man and Heavenly Principle should be united, but he could not persistently hold this view. In his opinion, the ideal way of conduct should be: "In everything there exists Principle of oughtness, but it has no relation with self." (*Academic Cases of the Confucian Scholars in the Ming Dynasty*, vol.1) "Existence of Principle of oughtness" means consciously regulating the conduct of the subject with Heavenly Principle; "no relation with self" means exclusion of the subject's will, demand, etc. This view about conduct is basically the direct continuation of Chengs-Zhu's theory.

Chen Xianzhang occupied an even more important position in the evolution of the Principlism of the Ming Dynasty. In contrast to Xue Xuan and Hu Juren's identification with the Chengs-Zhu's philosophy, Chen Xianzhang's thought was much closer to Lu Jiuyuan's. Like Lu Jiuyuan, Chen Xianzhang raised Mind to a prominent position: "The Mind of a superior man is full of all Principles. Although there are all things in the world, are they not in my Mind?" (*The Complete Works of Baishazi*, vol.2) Here, two relations are involved, i.e. between Mind and Principle, and between self and thing. As to the relation between Mind and Principle, all Principles existed in Mind, and Mind determined all Principles; as to the relation between self and thing, all things of creation were embodied in self, and outside self there was nothing. They unfolded the views in Lu Jiuyuan's Mindology from different aspects. With the above-mentioned views as the starting point, Chen Xianzhang thought that the primary thing for a scholar to do was to "study Mind", while the physical practice of Mind study was meditation. It had no involvement with study efforts, such as reading, discussion, etc.; neither did it have any concern with moral practice, such as service of a monarch or one's parents. This advocacy of Mind study through meditation not only pushed the view of "no Principle outside Mind" to the extreme, but also lead the cultivation of the Confucian inner sagehood to the way of dull emptiness.

In conclusion, after the end of the Southern Song Dynasty, Principlists expounded and elucidated respectively the Principlism of Chengs-Zhu School and Lu Jiuyuan's Mindology. However, in theoretical development, they did not make any fundamental breakthrough from Zhu's Principlism and Lu's Mindology; instead, they usually aggravated the internal theoretic weaknesses in the two systems. This course of evolution of Principlism from the end of the Southern Song Dynasty to the first half of the Ming Dynasty demonstrated that it was not a theoretical solution to waver between Zhu and Lu: history called for new philosophical thinking. It is such historical background of the evolution of Principlism that gave rise to Wang Yangming's Mindology unfolded in *Records of the Instructions and Reviews*.

Chapter Two

Records of the Instructions and Reviews and Wang Yangming's Mindology

1. From *Records of the Instructions and Reviews* to *The Complete Works of Yangming*

Wang Yangming was born in the eighth year (1472) of the Chenghua Period of the Ming Dynasty and died in the seventh year (1529) in the reign of Emperor Jiajing. His name is Shouren, and alias Bo'an. His ancestral hometown is in Yuyao, Zhejiang, and his father moved to live in Shanyin. He once studied and lectured in the Yangming Cave near Yuecheng, and he was known as Yangming since then.

Life stories of philosophers are usually quite plain, although their thoughts can be "superbly brilliant" and produce shocking intellectual powers. In philosophical meditation, they usually live a tranquil and simple life in their studies. Immanuel Kant can be a good example in this aspect. The philosopher indeed evoked a Copernican revolution in his realm. However, in all his life, he had almost never left Königsberg, the town he lived in. He lived a mechanical life like a clock, which seemed to constitute the classical pattern of the modern academic philosophers. In contrast with this kind of philosophers, Wang Yangming lived an extraordinary life. As a philosopher, he had certainly experienced the enlightenment at Longchang after his philosophical meditation. However, his meditation was not accomplished in a cozy and tranquil study, and more often he suffered hardships in life, which tortured his heart and tempered his will, and was banished to the remote borderland where savage minorities lived. Wang

Yangming's course of philosophical pursuit was closely connected with his tortuous life from his initial vague interest in philosophy in his early years to the philosophical summation in his late life. To a great extent, it was correspondingly an integrated course of his study, his pursuit of the Way, and his conduct as a man.

Wang Yangming took an interest in some philosophical issues of the ultimate significance in his childhood. At 12, he asked his private tutor an unusual question: "What is the top priority for a man?" The tutor thought it should be nothing but the success in the imperial civil examination. Wang Yangming disapproved of the answer. In his mind, the true top priority for a man should be to "follow the examples of sages and superior men through learning". "To follow examples of sages and superior men" meant that he would strive to attain inner sagehood as his life goal. As he gradually grew mature in thought, this top priority to attain inner sagehood became increasingly his conscious pursuit. It is right on this problem of how to attain sagehood that he made long-time exploration, and the results were recorded in his quotations, letters on study, etc. Some of his disciples later edited his quotations and letters that could demonstrate his academic purports, as well as other writings, into the *Records of the Instructions and Reviews*.

Records of the Instructions and Reviews consists of three volumes altogether. The materials of the first part in the first volume were collected by Xu Ai, Wang Yangming's younger sister-in-law and later his student. In the course of Wang Yangming's talks on study, Xu Ai recorded the discussions about Mind, Nature, relation between knowledge and action, etc., and compiled them into a book entitled *Records of the Instructions and Reviews*. Unfortunately Xu Ai died young, and what he recorded was only a small part. About the same time or a little later, Wang Yangming's other two students, Xue Kan and Lu Yuan, also recorded and edited what Wang Yangming lectured regularly. In 1516, Xue Kan compiled his, Xu Ai's, and Lu Yuan's collected quotations of Wang Yangming on study into one volume, entitled it *Records of the Instructions and Reviews*, and published it in block-printed edition. It is the first volume of the present book of *Records of the Instructions and Reviews.*

The second volume of the book was edited by Wang Yangming's another student Nan Daji. It was published with the title of *A Block-printed Sequel to Records of the Instructions and Reviews*, as a continuation of Xue Kan's edition of *Records of the Instructions and Reviews*. The second volume included mainly Wang Yangming's letters on learning, such as the famous "Reply to Gu Dongqiao", "Reply to Lu Yuanjing", "Reply to Ouyang Chongyi", "Reply to Vice Minister Luo Zheng'an", "Teaching Regulations", etc. These letters were all written by Wang Yangming himself and directly reflected his thoughts. As far as the contents are concerned, they covered the straightforward exposition of the theory of knowledge and action, the theory of innate knowledge, the theory of attainment of innate knowledge, etc., and also his responses and refutations to the relevant criticisms and reproaches of the contemporary scholars. They demonstrated the different aspects of Wang Yangming's thought.

When the first two volumes were published in block-printed editions, Wang Yangming was still alive. After his death, his brilliant disciple, Qian Dehong[1], widely solicited his posthumous works and quotations among his students, and gradually accumulated quite a number of important texts. From the answers to academic questions and the quotations provided by many of Wang Yangming's students, Qian Dehong made some selections, edited the most essential parts into *A Sequel to Records of the Instructions and Reviews*, and had it block-printed and published. It became the third volume of the present book. As far as the contents are concerned, it is close to the first volume of *Records of the Instructions and Reviews*. The third volume is a collection of Wang Yangming's quotations, including some important expositions in his late years (for instance, the four-sentence instruction), and several well-known discussions between Wang Yangming and his disciples on Mindology, such as Verification of the Way on the Tianquan Bridge, Dialogue at Yantan, etc.

---

[1] Qian Dehong (1496 – 1574), a notable philosopher, writer, and educator of the Ming Dynasty. An early student of Wang Yangming, Qian collected and emended Wang's philosophical works; after Wang's death, he edited Wang's biography.

Although the three volumes are not in great length, *Records of the Instructions and Reviews* provides a panorama of Wang Yangming's Mindology in a fairly thorough fashion. In practice, it collected his theories and expositions in a period of intellectual maturity. In terms of the contents, it covers almost all the aspects of Wang Yangming's Mindology. From the distinction between Mind and Nature, to the relation between Mind and things; from the theory of attainment of innate knowledge, to the theory of noumenon and effort; from unity of knowledge and action, to oneness of all things of creation: all these issues are included in the propositions of the book. The main purports and intellectual tendencies of his Mindology can also be basically learned in the book. In a sense, *Records of the Instructions and Reviews* constitutes the main body of Wang Yangming's Mindology.

Besides the book, Wang Yangming's disciples and descendants also edited some of his other writings and published them successively, such as *Master Yangming's Writings* and *A Sequel to Master Yangming's Writings* edited and printed by Qian Dehong, etc., and *The Family History of Master Yangming* by his heir-son Wang Zhengyi. In 1572, Xie Tingjie, an imperial censor, collected the three volumes of *Records of the Instructions and Reviews* and Wang Yangming's other posthumous works, as well as *The Chronological Biography of Wang Yangming* edited by his disciples, and compiled them into *The Complete Works of Literary Master Wang*, altogether in 38 volumes. The different editions of Wang Yangming's complete works published in later years were mainly based on this edition. Through the Ming and Qing Dynasties, this edition was continuously carved and printed, and in 1936, his complete works were again typeset, printed and published by Zhonghua Book Company in the title of *The Complete Collection of Yangming*. From *The Complete Works of Literary Master Wang* to *The Complete Collection of Yangming*, it was a long course of inheritance. No matter how this edition has evolved, the core of Wang Yangming's thought in his works has always been in *Records of the Instructions and Reviews*, and it is first through *Records of the Instructions and Reviews* that Wang Yangming's Mindology exerted wide influence.

2. Reconstruction of Mind-Body

Wang Yangming held that attainment of sagehood was the top priority for himself, and this determined his way of thinking was directed foremostly toward internal Mind and Nature. In a broader theoretical background, the distinction between Mind and Nature logically made it possible for Principlism to solve the problem of attaining inner sagehood. It is because of this approach that Principlism is usually regarded as a philosophy of Mind and Nature. In this aspect, Wang Yangming's Mindology did not leave the theoretic domain of Principlism. Of course, there existed important differences between Wang Yangming's Mindology and the Principlism of the Chengs-Zhu's School as to the views of Mind and Nature, and the positioning of the relation between Mind and Nature.

As related above, what Chengs-Zhu emphasized is firstly Nature as universal essence. In contrast to Chengs-Zhu's emphasis on Nature, Wang Yangming seemed to put more emphasis on Mind. He stressed repeatedly, "The study of the sage is the study of Mind," and his philosophy is also usually called Mindology. The Mind Wang Yangming referred to has a broad sense, including perception, thinking, feeling, intention, etc. In the perspective of learning and pursuit of the Way, attention should be paid primarily to the concept of Mind-Body. Wang Yangming demanded repeatedly "efforts on Mind-Body". (*The Complete Works of Wang Yangming*, Shanghai Classics Press, 1992, 14, briefly *Complete Works* hereafter) Mind as Body manifests in one aspect the difference of Wang Yangming's Mindology from Chengs-Zhu's philosophy.

As for the connotation of Mind-Body, Wang Yangming defined it in multiple aspects. First, he connected Mind with Principle, and held that Mind not only was a perceptual existence (not just a blood and meat ball), but also possessed Principle as its internal stipulation. The infiltration of Principle endowed Mind with mutually-related dual qualities, i.e. innateness and universal necessity. Innateness reflected the aspect that Mind existed before experience, and it is right in this sense that Wang

Yangming maintained: "Mind is possessed at birth." (*Complete Works*, 976) Universal necessity represented the aspect that Mind transcended specific time and space, as Wang Yangming said: "There is no separation between Heaven and Man, and no division between past and present."

Through defining Mind with Principle, Wang Yangming introduced transcendental moral law into Mind-Body. In its static state, Mind manifested itself as the moral law of universal necessity; and in its dynamic state, Mind again demonstrated itself as a legislator in the domain of moral practice (i.e. promulgator of moral orders). The latter represents the dominance of Mind: "It is because of its concentrated dominance that it is called Mind." (*Records of the Instructions and Reviews*, vol.2) In view of the idea that Principle was taken as the Body of Mind and understood mainly as the universal moral law, Wang Yangming's line of thinking does not have any essential difference from that of Chengs-Zhu's. However, Chengs-Zhu rarely talked about the meaning of the dominance of Mind but emphasized the dominance of Principle. Zhu Xi criticized Buddhism: "It only held Mind as dominant; therefore, it is inevitable to become selfish." In Chengs-Zhu's school, the focus of attention is mainly on how to adapt Mind to Principle, not on promulgating moral laws from Mind. In other words, dominance of Principle in Mind prevails over independence of Mind.

Chengs-Zhu demanded transformation of Mind into Nature and "temper Feeling with Nature"; the relation between Mind and Nature was manifested as exposition of Mind with Nature, that is, to define individual Mind with universal Nature. This line of thinking focused more on connecting the innateness of Mind with its transcendence, but did not pay due attention to the experiential contents of Mind. On the contrary, Wang Yangming emphasized the innate origin of Mind (received from Heaven), and at the same time did not direct his attention to transcendence. When his disciple Chen Jiuchuan asked about the ways to reach a peaceful state, he answered: "Why do you search for Heavenly Principle beyond your Mind? That is exactly the obsession with Principle." (*Records of the Instructions and Reviews, Complete Works*, vol.3, 92) Principle beyond Mind was the transcendental Principle. Regarding the search for Principle beyond Mind as obsession with Principle can be viewed as a criticism of Chengs-Zhu's theory. Differing from this transcendental approach of searching for Principle beyond Mind, Wang Yangming affirmed that Mind-Body possessed innate and universal Principle of necessity, and at the same time he again connected it with experiential contents and sensitive existence. He affirmed, "Therefore if there is no Mind, there is no physical body," meanwhile he stressed, "If there is no physical body, there is no Mind." Physical body is a sensitive existence. Although Mind cannot be equal to physical body of blood and flesh, it is not an existence separated completely from sensitive ears, eyes, mouth, nose, etc. Acceptance of the connection between Mind and physical body, of course, cannot be regarded as a unique view; however, in contrast with Chengs-Zhu's exposition of Mind with Nature, it is indeed a point worth noting. If it can be said that exposition of Mind with Nature was intended to separate Mind from sensitive existence and experiential contents, then the theory that "No body, no Mind" aims at reaffirmation of the relation between Mind and sensitivity.

At the level of consciousness, perceptual existence always involves experiential contents. Inseparability of Mind from physical body (No body, no Mind) determines that it is impossible for Mind to be separated completely from experiential contents. When talking about the relation between Mind and Feeling, Wang Yangming affirmed this point: "Joy, anger, sadness, fear, love, disgust, and desire are called the seven feelings. They all exist innately in Mind of every man." (*Records of the Instructions and Reviews*, vol.3) In contrast with intelligent apperception of Principlism, Feeling belongs to the order of perceptual experience. Wang Yangming regarded the seven feelings as indispensible meanings in the topic of Mind of Man, and at the same time, it denotes a connection between innate Mind-Body and experiential contents. In Wang Yangming's theory, this connection between Mind and Feeling is not just an occasional expression. In fact, Wang Yangming regarded happiness as noumenon of Mind, and believed: "Happiness is the noumenon of Mind." In a broad sense, happiness can be divided into sensual pleasure and spiritual enjoyment. The real happiness of the sage and the superior man, as mentioned by Principlists, stressed the side of spiritual enjoyment. But both sides of happiness — sensual pleasure and spiritual enjoyment — were mixed with some emotional factors. Not to mention sensual pleasure (for in instinctive pleasure already exists the feeling of like or dislike), even spiritual enjoyment alone had already exceeded pure sensation, but after all spiritual enjoyment was different from abstract rational knowledge or logic speculation, for right from the beginning, it embodied emotional recognition. Kong Zi demanded that love of benevolence be like that of good colors. Love of benevolence was the love of benevolent Principle (affirmation of benevolent Principle). Love of good colors (love of beautiful colors) was a natural acceptance of emotions. That is to say, the spiritual enjoyment (love of benevolence) that originated from benevolent spirit tends to attain perfection only when one had such emotional recognition like love of beautiful colors. In this sense, there existed a relative distinction between sensual pleasure and spiritual enjoyment: both to a certain extent contained some experiential contents.

Ever since Zhou Dunyi, discussion of "Kong-Yan's happiness" became a favorite topic for Principlists. In Chengs Zhu's orthodox Principlism, "Kong-Yan's happiness" was mainly understood as a rationalized spiritual concept in opposition to sensual feeling. Disagreeing with this view, Wang Yangming stressed that happiness of noumenon was not outside happiness of the seven feelings when he made a distinction between happiness of noumenon of Mind and happiness of the seven feelings. The seven feelings as human emotion should always benefit from natural expression. The third volume of *Records of the Instructions and Reviews* recorded: "Question: 'Happiness is noumenon of Mind. I wonder whether it still exists when one wails over great misfortune.' The master answered: 'Happiness should come after the wail, and there is no happiness without the wail. After the wail, Mind becomes tranquil, and that is happiness, but noumenon remains unchanged.'" (*Complete Works*, 112) Happiness here is no longer a special mood in a narrow sense (in opposition to sadness or bitterness), but generally refers to the usual emotional experience of the subject. Emotions are often restrained internally or externally, such as when one wants to cry but cannot, or he is sorrowful but suppresses it. These can be regarded as emotional distortion under pressure. In the cases that one expresses his sorrow when he is sorrowful, and wails at the moment he should cry, the subject can feel real enjoyment of emotional vexation. Here happiness lies in the natural outlet and expression of internal pent-up emotions without repression and distortion under pressure. It can be seen that the theoretic implication with happiness as noumenon of Mind lies foremostly in avoiding the excessive pressure of emotion and giving it an appropriate position in the subjective consciousness.

In a word, the Mind-Body Wang Yangming defined is not only based on Principle, but also connected with physical body and embedded with a dimension of perception. In the sense of the former, Mind and Nature are connected in one aspect; in the sense of the latter, Mind is not restricted only to Nature: the noumenon of happiness within the seven feelings is very difficult to be included into the noumenon of rationalized nature. Principle as a basis determines apriority (transcendence) of Mind, and connection with perceptual existence makes Mind unable to be isolated completely from experience. Thus, Mind-Body on the whole represents a blend of transcendental form and experiential contents, and Principlism and non-Principlism.

Wang Yangming's above understanding of Mind-Body has of course affinities to Lu Jiuyuan's Mindology, yet the two are not completely the same. Although Lu Jiuyuan exalted Mind to a prominent position, there is a dual tendency in his understanding of Mind-Body. This duality prevented Lu Jiuyuan from eliminating the internal tension in his Mindology. In comparison, Wang Yangming understood Mind-Body as a unity of transcendental form and experiential contents, and Principlism and non-Principlism. It seems that he made some progress in solving the internal tension of Lu Jiuyuan's Mindology.

Of course, in the perspective of the development of the Confucian theory of Mind and Nature, Wang Yangming's way of thinking is especially characteristic in a comparison with Chengs-Zhu's thought. As mentioned above, Chengs-Zhu on the whole preferred to expound Mind with Nature. In their original sense, when Nature was opposed to Mind, it mainly represented Principlist essence of Man. Exposition of Mind with Nature or transformation of Mind into Nature was thus intended for establishing the dominant position of Principlist noumenon. Principlist essence is one of the universal essences of Man that are different from other existences, so Chengs-Zhu emphasized that Nature was Principle, and stressed the distinction of Man from other existences on the level of Principlism. However, excessive emphasis on Principlistic noumenon can often easily cause the understanding of Man per se as abstract existence. When Zhu Xi demanded purification of Mind of Man with Mind of the Way, he more or less ignored the rich definitions of Man in reality, and regarded Man as the incarnation of Principlism in a one-sided view. From this starting point, it will be very difficult for the diversified development of Man to be put into practice: The priority of Principlism is inclined to restrain the attention on the dimensions of existence, and emotion, will, intuition, etc. It is right from here that Chengs-Zhu oriented their thought towards essentialism. In comparison with this tendency, Wang Yangming affirmed Principle as noumenon of Mind, and at the same time he also expounded Mind in connection with physical body and held Feeling, will and happiness as due meanings of Mind. There is no doubt that he paid more attention to the contents in multiple aspects of subjective consciousness, and multiple definitions of Man's existence. The latter in theory provided the prerequisites for the theory of Mind and Nature in affirmation of Man's individuality and the diversified development of individuality.

As related before, Chengs-Zhu's approach of expounding Mind with Nature in theory demonstrated the inclination toward a blend of innateness and transcendence: Noumenon of Nature was not only a priori, but also transcendental. Once the noumenon of Principlism is endowed with a transcendental attribute, it will usually be transformed into a heteronymous and compulsory force. In Zhu Xi's theory, the relation between Mind of the Way and Mind of Man implied compulsion, as he demanded Mind of Man submit to Mind of the Way. In other words, it is that Mind of the Way gave absolute order to Mind of Man. In contrast, Wang Yangming based his theory on Mind-Body, and understood it as a unity of innate form and experiential content, and of Principlism and non-Principlism. This indeed manifests a different way of thinking, and undoubtedly has a theoretical significance that cannot be overlooked in solving the tensions between transcendence and experience, Principlism and non-Principlism, Mind of the Way and Mind of Man, and in checking the excessive dominance of Principlism. In the perspective of intellectual development from the middle to the late Ming Dynasty, the above-mentioned thought of Wang Yangming indeed exerted remarkable influence on the ideas that emphasized the individual existence and rebellion against the essentialist trend.

In the meantime, Wang Yangming connected innate noumenon with perceptual existence, which, to some extent, provided the latent possibility of discarding apriority of noumenon. Logically, apriority of noumenon can lead to two aspects: from apriority to transcendence, and to the end of restricting and going beyond apriority through the connection of innateness and experience. Certainly Wang Yangming did not complete the latter course, but he connected the function of Mind-Body with perceptual activity, etc., and provided certain prerequisite for the completion of this course. It is along the above line of Wang Yangming's thought that Huang Zongxi[①] further proposed: "There is no noumenon of Mind, and attainment of effort is noumenon." (Preface to *Academic Cases of Confucian Scholars in the Ming Dynasty*) The purport here is that Mind-Body was not a fait accompli or an innate existence, but formed and developed in the cognitive process of real life. This view has transcended the transcendental speculative domain, and reached a historical and more realistic understanding of Mind-Body (subjective consciousness). The intellectual source of the latter can be traced back to the separation between apriority and transcendence.

---

① Huang Zongxi (1610 – 1695), a Confucian scholar, historian, philosopher, and naturalist at the end of the Ming Dynasty into the early Qing Dynasty. He is regarded as one of the most important enlightenment thinkers of China.

Wang Yangming moved from noumenon of Nature to Mind-Body, and to a certain extent, his course of thinking is manifested as a return to the thought of Meng Zi from Chengs-Zhu's theory. In terms of the internal structure of his philosophical system, the reconstruction of Mind-Body again constituted the logical prerequisite of his theory of personality and of Moral Nature. In accordance with his affirmation of the universal Principle embodied in Mind-Body, Wang Yangming stressed that the realm of personality had its aspect of loftiness and universality; in connection with the stress on the definition of individuality in Mind-Body, Wang Yangming repeatedly emphasized: "A man should achieve success according to his own talent." (*Records of the Instructions and Reviews*, vol.1) In his view, individuality of Man differed from person to person; therefore, it could not be possible to seek uniformity by imposing a general model. With regard to the goal, individual development had the tendency towards identity (with attainment of sagehood as the ultimate ideal), but the ways to the ideal realm could be different. Cultivation of personality should be based on characteristics of each individual, and adopt corresponding forms. In view of practical state, individuality consisted of contents of multiple aspects. If individuality was only constrained with universal Principlist norms, individuals' development of creativity and internal vitality would unavoidably be hindered, and personality formed under this condition would often become an embodiment of abstract criteria of Principlism. Chengs-Zhu based their theory on noumenon of Nature, and focused their attention firstly on shaping individuals with universal Principle, that is, guaranteeing loftiness and universality of personality with Principlist noumenon, but it often could not avoid neglecting the criterion of individuality in the cultivation of personality. Wang Yangming regarded Mind-Body as the starting point for attainment of sagehood. This kind of starting point logically contains the criterion of "achieving success according to individual talent". Therefore, Wang Yangming opposed compulsory education of people "in a general model", which, more or less, transcended the assimilation of individualistic Principle with abstract Principlist guideline.

Internality of ideal personality is not only linked with individual existence but also directs to sincerity in a deeper sense. Inner sagehood as an ideal realm of personality is not an external ornament, but a sincere character of self-substantiation. If one only abides by external norms, and cannot combine the general Principlist guideline with the internal noumenon of Mind, then his conduct will usually be like the performance of an actor: "If a man does not have a sincere Mind, although he inquires about his parents' health and pays respect to them every day, he is just acting like an actor, and it is not filial piety. This shows that sincerity of Mind is the Heavenly Principle." (*Complete Works*, 1174-5) Performance is always for show. Although actors can imitate the characters in real life, after all the performance is different from the real personality in life. Attainment of sagehood means reaching perfection. If during the course a man only conducts himself by making different gestures (for instance inquiring about his parents' health everyday only superficially), i.e. in pursuit of Principlist norms in external form, then it is just like the performance of a play, and it is difficult to realize a true personality. In Wang Yangming's view, in order to avoid such an external ornament, it was a must to assimilate universal Principle into Mind-Body, and transform external norms into internal morality, so that one would conduct himself not only in the formalized Principlist norms (rituals), but from the true internal moral noumenon.

It can be seen that in Wang Yangming's view, construction of Mind-Body was closely related with whether one could attain inner sagehood. Wang Yangming interpreted Mind-Body as the unity of universal Principle and individual Mind, while this moral noumenon again constituted the internal basis for attainment of sagehood: If Principle as the definition of universality in Mind-Body guaranteed loftiness of the realm of internal sagehood, then the blend of Mind and Principle (Principle was internalized into Mind) provided the guarantee for the transformation of internal sagehood into a true self-substantiated sincere personality. The two from different aspects explained in theory how internal sagehood could become possible.

Mind-Body as a unity of Principlism and non-Principlism, universality and individuality, has certain ontological significance: It always coexists with the subject in reality. In other words, Mind-Body is not a logic form without personality. It exists in a subject in all his course of life, and internal sagehood as perfect morality constitutes the realm of the subject. The ontological significance of Mind-Body also logically determines the ontological significance of the realm of internal sagehood: The true realm is always transformed into the concrete existence of Man, and unfolds in the course of Man's practice. Thus, the unity of Mind-Body and internal sagehood, at the same time, implies the unity of existence and realm. Wang Yangming emphasized the connection between universal Principle and individual existence, and indeed paid more attention to the realistic quality of moral noumenon and moral realm.

In correspondence with this kind of realistic dimension of noumenon, the blend of Principle and Mind means a return from the metaphysical domain of transcendence to the individual existence in a certain extent. Wang Yangming connected the metaphysical domain with the physical domain, and Principlism with sensibility, with his theory that "Mind was Principle", and regarded it as the internal noumenon for the realization of the ideal realm. This line of thinking not only paid attention to the connection between existence and essence, but also affirmed correspondingly the perceptual definition in ideal personality. Therefore, it more or less avoided delving into abstractness and one-sidedness.

3. Mind and Thing

Mind-Body as noumenon is not just limited to subjective consciousness; right from the beginning, it has been related with existence in a broad sense. The reconstruction of Mind-Body correspondingly provides a logical prerequisite for the study of the relation between Mind and Thing. In this relation, Wang Yangming's interest did not rest on the provision of a certain metaphysical cosmological mode or a picture of the world, but on the connection of the definition of existence with the construction of the world of meaning. The latter represents a unique theoretic orientation.

Wang Yangming once put forward a famous proposition, namely, "Where there is a meaning, there is a thing." (*Records of the Instructions and Reviews*, vol.1) Here the meaning is a form of expression of Mind-Body in the course of activity. Thing is different from natural existence because natural existence is always outside subjective consciousness (not used by the subject). A thing as "where there is a meaning" is an existence that has been activated by subjective consciousness and has entered the domain of subjective consciousness. A meaning in a thing is not only a course of intention (meaning directed to the object), but also a course in which the subject gives meaning to the object. In Wang Yangming's view, if a man lacked ethical and political consciousness, then for him, dear ones (parents), monarch, people, etc. only existed as general objects and were not different from natural objects of mountains, rivers, grass and trees, etc.; only when Mind-Body was directed to parents, monarch, people, etc. could they be regarded as "parents", "monarch" and "people", etc., in ethical and political relations presented in the subject; that is, the subject then obtained meanings of "parents", "monarch", "people", etc.

It can be seen that that "Where there is a meaning, there is a thing" is not that consciousness constructs a material world in the external space, but that consciousness through externalization of Mind-Body (activity of intention) gives existence a meaning and thus constructs a meaningful world of the subject. Nothingness outside Mind does not mean that the original object (natural object) cannot exist outside Mind-Body, but that the existence of the world of meaning into the domain of consciousness can always have real meaning only in relation to the subject. It is not difficult to discover that this world of meaning is different from the metaphysical world of noumenon: It is not a transcendental existence, but firstly takes form and unfolds itself in the subject's conscious activity, and has close relation with the existence of Man himself. Wang Yangming indeed manifested a different line of thinking in restricting his scope of study within the world of meaning in contrast with Chengs-Zhu's speculative construction of existence from the perspective of cosmology and in the logic relation between Principle and *qi*. That, in a sense, can be regarded as a change of ontological orientation.

Of course, the world of meaning is not merely represented as a product of intentional activity. In Wang Yangming's theory, the course in which the meaning was directed to the object was at the same time a course of practice to serve parents and work for monarch. As an intention of Mind, meaning first started in moral practice, and when there was a meaning, it also existed first in the course of this kind of practice. Therefore, Thing was not only a static object, but was closely connected with the subject's activity. In fact, in Wang Yangming's theory, Thing and Matter were already exchangeable: Matter was often understood as Thing, as expressed in "Matter is Thing". When meaning was directed to original Matter, indeed it transformed original existence into the object in the world of meaning, but at this time the world of meaning was still mainly an existence of consciousness. Only through practical course could the world of meaning further obtain its quality of reality. Thus, intention and actual practice had an internal connection. Meaning was directed to the object and caused original existence to obtain a humanized meaning (for instance, natural blood relation between parents and children becomes an object in an ethical sense), while the moral practice to serve parents and work for monarch constituted in reality the ethical relations between parents and children, and between monarch and subject. The connection between Matter and Thing caused the emphasis of Mindology to turn from the transcendental "Thing itself" to the object in practice, and the blend of intentional activity and moral practice allowed the construction of the world of meaning to no longer manifest itself as mere activity in the domain of consciousness.

What has been covered above is mainly the domain of morality. The world of meaning is definitely not just an ethical world, for it has more extensive connotations. When talking about the relation between innate knowledge and heaven, earth and all things of creation, Wang Yangming proposed: "Innate knowledge is the spirit of Nature. These spirits can give birth to heaven and earth, and become ghosts and emperors. All things of creation are produced from it; indeed, it has no counterpart in the material world." (*Records of the Instructions and Reviews*, vol.3. *Complete Works*, 104) Here the generation of heaven and earth is not a relation of cosmological generation, but a relation of meaning between Mind-Body and object. Outside of Mind-Body, heaven and earth certainly still exist, but they are the original and undeveloped "beings". Division of heaven and earth, or presentation of heaven and earth in such existence, cannot be separated from the intelligent apperception of Mind-Body (innate knowledge). That "All things of creation are produced from it" means that the meanings of "heaven" and "earth" originate from Mind-Body (given by Mind-Body). In view of this kind of relation of meaning, Mind and Matter are not represented as two opposite orders: Matters like heaven, earth, etc., in the world of meaning are difficult to be separated from Mind-Body (innate knowledge). Outside of Mind-Body, heaven and earth are no longer represented as "heaven and earth" in the world of meaning. In this sense, the two indeed were "not counterparts" at all.

Wang Yangming's above views were not widely understood among his contemporaries, and even his disciples from time to time questioned him. The third volume of *Records of the Instructions and Reviews* recorded a story as follows: Wang Yangming and several disciples went outing in the mountains. One of them pointed at the mountain flowers in full bloom on the rocks and said: "These flowers in the deep mountains blossom and wither by themselves. What kind of relation do they have with my Mind-Body?" Wang Yangming replied: "When you do not see the flowers, the flowers and your Mind are both lonely and silent. When you come to see the flowers, the colors of the flowers all appear bright and white. Therefore it can be known that the flowers are not outside of your Mind." The disciple asked a question that had a different focus from Wang Yangming's definition of existence. Here the idea about Mind and flowers both in loneliness and silence is left for later discussion. The perception of the flowers that blossom and wither by themselves focuses on their natural existence, while whether the colors of the flowers are bright and white or not is related to the subject who sees them. In view of natural existence, the blossoming and withering of flowers seems to have nothing to do with Mind-Body, but considering what kind of form the flowers are represented, i.e. what kind of meaning the flowers have to the subject after all, it is very difficult to say that it has no relation with Mind-body: Whether the colors of the flowers are fresh and bright or not has already involved the aesthetic form of flowers. This form is not a natural existence, and it is only meaningful to a subject with aesthetic ability. It is right as Karl Marx pointed out: "To those ears without a sense of music, the best music is also meaningless." (*Manuscripts of Economics and Philosophy of 1844*, People's Publishing House, 1985, 82) Wang Yangming said: "These flowers are not outside of your Mind," and it seems he meant emphatically the above relation of meaning.

Existence in the relation of meaning is certainly not limited to the aesthetic form of flowers. Broadly speaking, it also exists in the relation between Man, and heaven and earth, and all things of creation: "My intelligence is the master of heaven, earth, ghosts and spirits. If heaven is not related to my intelligence, who will look up at its loftiness? If earth is not related to my intelligence, who will look down into its depth?" (*Records of the Instructions and Reviews*, vol.3) In the same way as innate knowledge that "gives birth to heaven and earth", the dominance here does not mean that "my intelligence" can determine existence, movement and change of heaven, earth and all things of creation, but that when the original existence of heaven, earth and all things of creation becomes the existence in the world of meaning, they cannot leave "I" and my conscious activity. As for "Thing as itself", there is no loftiness or lowness for heaven; only in relation to me, heaven appears lofty; without me, heaven certainly exists, but the loftiness in relation to me (its loftiness to me) no longer exists. As far as this is concerned, it can be said: "If heaven is not related to my intelligence, who will look up at its loftiness?"

Wang Yangming's above analysis and explanation of the world of meaning once caused perplexity among some of his disciples. Their doubt is expressed in the third volume of *Records of the Instructions and Reviews*: "Heaven and earth, and all things of creation have existed from antiquity to present, so why did you say that they did not exist without my intelligence?" To this question, Wang Yangming made the following reply: "If you saw a man who had passed away, his spirit and intelligence existed no longer. Where were his heaven and earth, and all things of creation?" (*Ibid.*) It is the same as the argument of whether the flowers that blossomed and withered by themselves had any relation with Mind: The above question is basically still on the standpoint of cosmology, and what it emphasized is original existence outside of Man. On the contrary, what Wang Yangming focused on was first "his" world, ("his heaven and earth, and all things of creation"). This kind of world is just the world of meaning that belongs to Man. Heaven, earth and all things of creation as natural existence do not exist or change at Man's will. However, the world of meaning always has its relative side. Heaven and earth, all things of creation, and different individuals usually constitute different meaning relations; in other words, to different subjects, heaven, earth and all things of creation often appear in different meanings. In some aspects, it seems that we can also say each man has a world that belongs to "him". When he reaches the end of his life, the world of meaning that belongs to him should also end at the same time. At this moment, it seems that Wang Yangming had the reason to ask back: "Where are his heaven and earth, and all things of creation?"

So far, Wang Yangming mainly emphasized the function of the subject (I) in the construction of the world of meaning. As a process, the formation of the world of meaning is not a fabrication out of nothing. In Chengs-Zhu's Principlism, the cosmological generation and development are usually expressed as unidirectional determination: the Ultimate of Extremity — *yin-yang* — five phases — all things of creation. In opposition to this, the construction of the world of meaning demonstrates different features. As related before, Wang Yangming once said: "Before you have seen the flowers, the flowers and your Mind both remain lonely and silent." Here "both remain lonely and silent" is very much worth noting. In view of the construction of the world of meaning, Mind is certainly the subject of function, while the world of meaning is the result of function, but the intentional activity of Mind-Body itself cannot be separated from its object; it is true that without Mind-Body there will be no way for the object to enter the world of meaning, but without the object, there will also be no way for Mind-Body to function: When the two have not met each other, both can only remain lonely and silent. In fact, the transformation of the original existence into the existence of the world of meaning is a change mainly in the way of the existence of the object, while this kind of change itself demands a prerequisite of the object that exists "in itself" to some extent. In this respect, the function of Mind-Body also depends on the world of objects to some extent.

It seems that Wang Yangming also noticed the above relation, and this can be found more or less in the following quotations: "If my intelligence is separated from heaven, earth, all things of creation, and ghosts and spirits, there will also not be my intelligence. If so, the two are mutually connected, and how can they be separated?" (*Records of the Instructions and Reviews,* vol.3) This seems to have a dual meaning that without heaven, earth, and all things of creation, there will be no "my intelligence". Firstly, in the meaning relation, Mind-Body and the object are inseparable; if there is no Mind-Body, certainly the object cannot become Thing in the world of meaning, without the object, Mind-Body (intelligence) is also no longer Mind-Body in the relation. Secondly, Mind-Body cannot fabricate anything completely out of nothing outside the physical world. Thus, Mind and Matter seem to have a mutual relation of substance and function: In the respect that only in the intentional activity can the object in itself be transformed into "my Thing" in the world of meaning, Mind is substance, and Thing is function; in the respect that if there are not heaven, earth, and all things of creation, there is also not "my intelligence", Thing is substance, and Mind is function. It is because of the meaning of the latter that Wang Yangming maintained: "Mind has no body, and its body can only be decided by whether there exists communion or not between Mind and heaven, earth and all things of creation." (*Ibid.*) That is to say, the activity of Mind itself also takes as its basis the mutual interaction between Mind and heaven, earth and all things of creation.

Wang Yangming's view on the relation between Mind and Thing

is often compared with the theory of George Berkeley, the noted Irish philosopher. Berkeley held that existence was being perceived. At first sight, it seems that his view bears much resemblance with Wang Yangming's "Where there is a meaning, there is a thing." However, on further examination, we may see that it is really difficult to say the two are simply the same. Berkeley's perception refers firstly to perception, but Wang Yangming's "meaning" is more complex in its connotation. As a form of expression of Mind-Body, it takes knowledge as its body, and again manifests itself as the intention of the subject; furthermore, there are also emotions, etc., that blend with knowledge and intention. Berkeley regarded perception as the first Principle, but perception as the first Principle of existence does not mainly manifest itself in the relation of meaning between perception and object, and its relation is existence or non-existence; in other words, in Berkeley's theory, perception was not mainly a condition for the possibility of meaning, but for the possibility of existence. He once cited an example: "The reason why the table I was writing at existed was because I could see it, and touch it." Here the point is not what kind of meaning the object (for instance, the table) appears to the subject, but whether the object itself exists or not. In contrast, Wang Yangming showed little interest in the problems of existence, non-existence, generation, etc., and what he focused on first is the relation of meaning between Mind-Body and the object. If Berkeley was still to construct existence in speculation by taking perception as the condition for the possibility of existence, then Wang Yangming turned from the construction of existence to that of the world of meaning.

It is usually very difficult to avoid metaphysical fabrication in the speculative construction of existence. Berkeley regarded "my perception" as the condition for possibility of existence, which implies in logic the following difficulty, i.e. it cannot be compatible with the fact of continuity of existence. If the existence of the object only depends on "my perception", then only when perception takes place, the object exists; when perception disappears, the object also no longer exists. In such a case, the object can only exist and disappear in constant intermittence, and is lacking continuity. In order to explain continuity of existence, Berkeley had to assume the existence of another subject of perception, and because of this, he further drew forth an "unlimited spiritual hypostasis": When I and other subjects had not perceived the object, the perception of the existence of the object still depended on "the unlimited spiritual hypostasis". Berkeley's transcendental supposition made it very difficult for his system to realize internal consistency theoretically: If the proposition that existence was being perceived was implemented to the end, the presupposition of unlimited spiritual hypostasis could not be established. In fact, it is always difficult to overcome completely this kind of theoretic obstacle in the construction of existence in a speculative way. In regard to Wang Yangming's system of Mindology, because he turned his interest away from the problems of being, non-being, generation in cosmology, etc., to the world of meaning, the construction of the ultimate existence was already beyond his domain of concern. Therefore, he did not need to suppose a certain metaphysical entity beyond Mind-Body, and neither did he have to face the internal theoretic difficulty caused therein.

Certainly, Wang Yangming had his own problem in his orientation of studying existence. He focused on the world of meaning as his domain, and in his definition that "Where there is a meaning, there is a thing", he emphasized chiefly the function of Mind-Body in giving meanings. Between the meaning world as function and Mind as substance, Wang Yangming usually paid more attention to the function of the latter (Mind-Body) in the construction of the former (the world of meaning). Because of this, object in itself was often accorded less attention. In fact, an object in the world of meaning is not only a "Thing in my Mind", but also an object in itself. When an object enters the meaning world, it is an existence in the meaning relation, but it is still not completely identical with the relation. Ignorance of the aspect that the object is also outside the relation (in itself) can often restrict it within the domain of consciousness. At the same time, when Wang Yangming connected Matter with Thing ("Matter is Thing"), he definitely noticed the connection between intentional activity and practical activity, but his regard of Thing as Matter also left no position for the object as a natural object. Since Wang Yangming based his theory on Mind-Body, it was very difficult for him to avoid the above prejudice in his theory.

4.   Innate Knowledge as Moral Nature

How to do good and eliminate evil in daily practice is one of the problems Principlism is concerned about. Doing good and eliminating evil entail distinction of good from evil as the prerequisite, and distinction of good from evil unfolds itself as a course of knowing (knowing good and evil). This kind of connection between moral conduct and moral knowledge can be found in the discussion and analysis of the early Confucian scholars. The statement "Without knowing, how can a man be benevolent?" (Kong Zi) implies such a point. Chengs-Zhu paid special attention to the relation between the two, and further emphasized the logical priority of knowing oughtness (command of universal norms) over conducting in accordance with oughtness (observance of norms in conduct). It is not difficult to see the tendency of thinking if we judge from the approach that Chengs-Zhu aimed at investigating all Principles under heaven. Here it seems to have implied some optimistic faith: The study of Principle of oughtness could logically lead to moral practice of doing good and eliminating evil.

Wang Yangming did not deny the significance of knowing oughtness over conducting in accordance with oughtness. Nevertheless, it seems that the relation between knowledge and morality was rather complex in his view. In talking about knowing evil and prohibiting evil, Wang Yangming wrote: "When a man is doing something immoral, it is not that his innate knowledge knows nothing about it; only because he can not attain his innate knowledge, in the end it is inevitable that he becomes an inferior man." Here the word "attainment" has the meaning of effort. When a man is doing evil, his moral consciousness might just as well be in an apperceptive state. In other words, he might just as well know what is good and what is evil. However, this knowing of good and evil does not naturally lead him to do good and evil. Obviously there exists some distance here between moral knowledge (knowledge of good) and moral conduct (conduct of good). The problem of how to do good and eliminate evil will be transformed concretely into how to apply knowledge of good and evil acquired in the course of learning into doing good and prohibiting evil in the course of practice.

Knowing good and evil is a course of rational cognition in a broad sense. What it mainly deals with is a question of "what it is", which covers the distinction between good and evil, the understanding of moral norms, the command of ethical relationships, etc. Although this kind of moral knowledge is different from general knowledge of facts, it still takes the existing reality as its objects (including the established norms, standards, ethical relationships, etc. in the domain of morality). In contrast, moral conduct primarily involves the problem of "what should be done". Logically speaking, between the knowledge of "what it is" and the requirement of "what should be done" does not exist an entailment relation: Knowing what it is cannot stipulate what should be done. How can one connect knowledge in cognition with conduct in practice? This is a question that cannot be avoided in moral philosophy. Wang Yangming held that knowing good and evil by oneself did not necessarily lead to doing good and prohibiting evil, and this at least in one aspect stressed the logical tension between knowing reality and doing in accordance with oughtness.

How can one proceed from knowing good to doing good? In Wang Yangming's theory, further questioning about this problem led to the consideration of the relation between the investigation of external objects and the realization of self intention. As related before, Chengs-Zhu began from the study of all Principles (a command of all Principles under heaven), which more or less implied the priority of knowledge in their thought. On the contrary, Wang Yangming focused his primary concern on how to realize self intention. In his exposition of "investigation of the objects of the world and acquirement of knowledge", he expressed his criticism of Chengs-Zhu. The term "investigation of the objects of the world and acquirement of knowledge" was put forward at first in the early

Confucian classic *The Great Learning*. During the Song and Ming Dynasties, philosophers offered various kinds of interpretation and elaboration on it. Zhu Xi usually understood it as the study of the objects of the physical world, but in Wang Yangming's view, the objects in the physical world were infinite, so how could they be studied one by one? Even if all the objects in the physical world were investigated and studied, how could one turn to himself and "realize self intention"? (*Records of the Instructions and Reviews*, vol.3) To perfect self intention means to perfect Moral Nature. In contrast, investigation of the objects of the world means more of the acquirement of knowledge. The former directs to the domain of oughtness as perfection of Moral Nature unfolds itself in the course of conduct in accordance with oughtness, while the latter aims at its implementation in reality. According to Wang Yangming's understanding, acquirement of knowledge and perfection of Moral Nature were two different orders. Accumulation of knowledge could not guarantee perfection of Moral Nature. "Even if one has a thorough study of grass and trees, how can one turn to himself and realize self intention?" The rhetorical question emphasized the logic distance between the two aspects. Here, the key of the problem does not lie in how to investigate all Principles under heaven, but in how to proceed from acquirement of knowledge to perfection of Moral Nature (realization of self intention).

The close connection between the perfection of Moral Nature (realization of self intention) and the domain of oughtness thus has a special significance in the transformation from knowing reality to doing in accordance with of oughtness: The logic prerequisite from knowing good and evil to doing good and prohibiting evil is to transform knowledge into Moral Nature. It is right in this meaning that Wang Yangming repeatedly stressed: "Pursuit of knowledge and inquiry is therefore veneration of Moral Nature." (*Ibid.*) "Veneration of Moral Nature" means the perfection of Moral Nature as the final goal. As the prerequisite of doing in accordance with oughtness, the perfection of Moral Nature (truthful intention, truthful self) is unfolded as a course of "self-substantiation". Self-substantiation means that through self-experience and practice, moral consciousness is transformed into internal Moral Nature of the subject. Wang Yangming made a distinction between "speaking with mouth and ears" and "speaking with body and Mind": Speaking with mouth and ears meant knowing the Way only through the means of "listening" and "speaking"; speaking with body and Mind meant truly experiencing the Way in personal practice. (*Records of the Instructions and Reviews*, vol.2) The Way and Heavenly Principle as objects of experience firstly refer to Principle of oughtness, and innate knowledge already embodies the moral Principlist Nature of knowing good and evil. There is no doubt that the understanding of good and evil and the knowledge of oughtness are meanings in the topics of Confucian study, but if they only exist in the state of knowledge, they still cannot dispossess their attribute of externality; only when it is blended into internal Moral Nature can innate knowledge become real existence of the subject: Even a deeper connotation for the difference between "speaking with mouth and ears" and "self-substantiation" is the division between external knowledge of Principlist Nature and internal, real Moral Nature.

It can be seen in Wang Yangming's view that the prerequisite for proceeding from knowing good to doing good was to transform knowledge into Moral Nature. This process at the same time means that through conduct and learning, innate knowledge as Principlist Nature in talking and discussion becomes self-substantiated real existence. As self-substantiated Moral Nature, innate knowledge constitutes the true self of the subject. This innate knowledge as the true self has already transcended rational distinction of knowing good and evil, and been blended with the existence of Man into one. It not only includes the apperception of oughtness, but has the intention of doing in accordance with oughtness: To know good and at the same time to like it just as one likes good colors; to know evil, and then to hate it just as one hates stinky smells; thus, both doing good and prohibiting evil will be adhered to regardless of oneself. The reason for it is because knowledge, like and hatred "all originate from true Mind". In the true Moral Nature, knowing good and doing good have become the relevant orientations of the same self, the opposition between speaking and commenting, and the contradiction between talking and doing begins to be sublated.

In the perspective of philosophical history, the distinction between knowledge and Moral Nature attracted the attention of philosophers at a very early time. Aristotle already began to differentiate technique from morality. The technique in his concept was mainly a kind of external knowledge. This externality was set in opposition to the subject; i.e. it possessed only the value of a tool, and had not been blended into the internal personality of self. Moral Nature was different from the external tool: It had been transformed into an inseparable part of the existence of the subject. When conduct was based on morality, the subject did not "apply" certain knowledge as a man manufactured a vessel, but regarded it as a way of his own existence. Starting from this point, some contemporary philosophers such as B. Williams further made distinction between truth of knowledge and truthfulness of morality. Truth of knowledge was firstly connected with consciousness of the object, while truthfulness of morality often involved introspective consciousness and mental set inside the subject. In this aspect, it seems that Wang Yangming's line of thinking is close to those of the above-mentioned philosophers. It was based on the distinction between external knowledge and internal Moral Nature as the prerequisite that he demanded the transformation of knowledge into Moral Nature, and regarded self-substantiated innate knowledge as real self (true self). He once criticized the singular emphasis on the external knowledge of writings, collation, techniques, etc., and held that if one only focused on them, certainly he could acquire knowledge which was restricted to external objects, and there was no way to perfect self. In Wang Yangming's mind, it was important to form internal Moral Nature of the subject through profound understanding of morality in experience.

True Moral Nature not only was the internal noumenon in the connection of moral knowledge with moral practice, but also determined Nature and the functional orientation of knowledge and conduct. In terms of knowledge, if there was no internal Moral Nature, then "More knowledge can be rightly applied to do evil." (*Records of the Instructions and*

Reviews, vol.2) In a general sense, knowledge is to some extent neutral in terms of values, and does not embody internally any functional orientation. It usually can either lead to doing good or doing evil. Even the knowledge of ethical domain (knowledge of oughtness, and knowledge of good and evil) may not necessarily lead to good conduct: It can also be used in hypocritical conduct. In comparison with pure knowledge, Moral Nature has already transcended the neutrality of value and acquired the orientation of goodness. At the same time, this Moral Nature of goodness, as a stable structure of consciousness, gradually becomes condensed as the personality of the subject and restrains the functional orientation of knowledge.

Likewise, Moral Nature also determines the nature of conduct. Whether there is a quality of goodness in the subject's conduct is determined by whether it comes out of truthful Moral Nature. As far as filial piety is concerned, "Truthful feeling of Mind in filial piety is Heavenly Principle. If a man truthfully pays respect to his parents and inquires about their health, even though he does not stand before their bed, still he is filial. If he has no truthful feeling, even though he pays respect to his parents and inquires about their health every day, it is not filial piety, but only similar to dramatic performance. It can be seen here that truthfulness of Mind is Heavenly Principle." (*Anecdotes to Records of the Instructions and Reviews, Complete Works*, 1174-5) Whether or not one's conduct can be judged as filial piety does not lie in formality, but in whether or not this conduct is based on the truthful Moral Nature. Without a truthful Moral Nature, even if a man performs different kinds of conduct, it is inevitably like dramatic performance and difficult to be accepted as the conduct of goodness.

Moral Nature as self-substantiated real existence is not an abstract noumenon. In Wang Yangming's view, it usually took innate knowledge as its concrete form. As mentioned before, innate knowledge can be interpreted differently. Chengs-Zhu emphasized that innate knowledge "originates from heaven, and has nothing to do with man." That is, it originated from the transcendental Heavenly Principle, and had no relation with self. At this level, innate knowledge exhibited itself more as an embodiment of universal Heavenly Principle, and not the true self. In the perspective of veneration of Moral Nature, Wang Yangming transformed the connotation of innate knowledge in theory, and moved it from the transcendental Principlism that had nothing to do with Man to individual existence. That true self was innate knowledge reflected this tendency. In this dimension of Moral Nature or true self, innate knowledge first acquired the form of self-criterion: "That bit of innate knowledge you have is your self-criterion." (*Records of the Instructions and Reviews*, vol.3) The criterion here often refers to the evaluation standards in the domain of values, and it first involves the evaluation of the judgment of good and evil. The evaluation of values naturally includes cognition, but it is different from general knowledge: The judgment of good and evil always involves the subject's balance, choice, will and orientation of value at the same time. In other words, the evaluation of values not only takes the knowledge of good and evil as its content, but also provides certain guides for conduct. Wang Yangming took innate knowledge as self-criterion, and at the same time affirmed the idea that internal Moral Nature could regulate and direct conduct.

Affirmation and rejection in the evaluation of values from the very beginning involve the dimension of emotions. Wang Yangming pinpointed this level of relation in the following statement: "Innate knowledge is only a Mind of affirmation and rejection. Affirmation and rejection are only a matter of like and dislike. Only like and dislike are the entire matter of affirmation and rejection. Only affirmation and rejection are the entire changes of all things of creation." (*Ibid.*) To like is to favor, and to dislike is to hate — both belong to the category of emotions in a broad sense. In the evaluation of good and evil, there exist not only rational distinction, but also identification of emotions: To like good and hate evil is not merely a pure rational judgment; moreover, it is an acceptance or rejection of feeling. Innate knowledge as transcendental Principlist Nature that had nothing to do with Man (in Chengs-Zhu's theory) can certainly keep far away from the domain of emotions, but when it is transformed into internal Moral Nature of the subject, it will be difficult to be isolated from emotions such as liking good and hating evil, etc. The dimension of emotions, embedded in Moral Nature, in one aspect constitutes the internal motivation of inclination to goodness, and also provides an opportunity for the transformation from knowing oughtness into doing in accordance with oughtness.

Besides the dimension of emotions, true Moral Nature also includes the definition of Will. Wang Yangming paid great attention to the function of Will, and regarded making determination as the prerequisite of moral conduct. Making determination is to determine the goal for conduct, and it is just like a helm of a boat that provides orientation for the subject's activity. If there is no determination, it means a man is aimless and at a loss what to do, and in the end he will inevitably accomplish nothing. This orienting function of will can also be regarded as intentionality in a broad sense. Of course, it possesses a quality of constancy and devotion; therefore, it is different from an ordinary occasional intention. As a constant and devoted intention, Will is always blended into Moral Nature and restrains the conduct of Man. Different from moral rationality that mainly tells people what good is and what evil is, the orientation of Will (orientation of intention) further demands people to choose good and reject evil. Through the influencing choice of conduct, Will constitutes another motivation for the transformation from knowing good to doing good.

The transition from moral knowledge to moral practice often faces the problem of weak will. "Although I know it is good, I cannot put it into practice; although I know it is evil, I still do it and cannot stop it." That is usually due to a lack of tenacious will. Thus, it always involves how to overcome weakness of will as to the transformation from knowing good and evil to doing good and eliminating evil. Right because of it, Wang Yangming, in his study of the relation between Will and conduct, specially mentioned "courage and devotion" of Will in the course of attainment of the Way. Devotion is to fix the direction of Will, and courage is the effort of Will; the latter expresses the firmness of Will. The advancement in the attainment of the Way can be regarded as the course of the realization of the moral ideal. How to transform an ideal into reality is in essence connected with how to proceed from knowing of oughtness to doing in accordance with oughtness, and both demand the quality of a firm Will as the prerequisite. Once a firm Will is formed, usually it will be further transformed into the orientation of conduct in inclining to doing good and rejecting evil, and will give the subject an internal strength so that he does not yield to external obstacles. This kind of firm Will with fixed orientation for conduct is of course not outside of self Moral Nature, since it has been condensed in innate knowledge and constitutes the internal definition of Moral Nature in the course of the moralization of innate knowledge. Therefore, the orientation of Will, at the same time, manifests the internal strength of innate knowledge (Moral Nature).

It is not difficult to notice that in Wang Yangming's theory, the transformation of knowledge into Moral Nature meant the transformation of self-obtained knowledge through a pursuit of advanced study into innate knowledge (transformation of the transcendental Principlist Nature that "has nothing to do with Man" into self-substantiated real self). As internal Moral Nature (true self), innate knowledge embodies the criteria and ability of self-evaluation, is unfolded as the emotional identification of doing good and hating evil, and restrains the choice and execution of conduct with constant intention and tenacious effort. This kind of Moral Nature not only blends with self-existence into one, but also constitutes a dynamic factor of the subject's conduct: The transformation from knowing good to doing good is based on the internal Moral Nature as its self dynamic factor, and the moral practice of doing good and rejecting evil is correspondingly manifested as a course based on self-discipline of subject.

Moral Nature as self-substantiated personality is an internal true self. But its internal formation does not mean that it is enclosed inside. Personality usually has its side of external manifestation, and Moral Nature is also often reflected in the course of conduct in reality. In connection with the transformation of knowledge into Moral Nature is the transformation of Moral Nature into moral conduct. With such an understanding, Wang Yangming at the same time affirmed the pursuit of knowledge and inquiry in order to venerate Moral Nature, and repeatedly demanded "accomplishment of moral conduct as purpose". (*Records of the Instructions and Reviews*, vol.2)

As far as the real course is concerned, perfection of Moral Nature and accomplishment of moral conduct are not isolated from each other. We can certainly examine the two respectively in logic, but in reality, the two are united in the life course of the same self. As the internal personality, Moral Nature always faces the problem of how to affirm itself. The self-affirmation of Moral Nature is not only a spiritual benefit, but also means a verification of self in moral conduct. Wang Yangming took filial piety and fraternity as example and explained: "When we say someone knows how to be filial to his parents and respect his brothers, we do not base our judgment on what he says about being filial to parents and respecting his brothers, but on his real conduct in accordance with the criteria." (*Records of the Instructions and Reviews*, vol.1) It is undoubtedly a manifestation of good Moral Nature in understanding filial piety and fraternity and having the intention to practice, but this kind of Moral Nature again must be manifested in the course of filial and fraternal conduct: It is the moral conduct of filial piety and fraternity that provides the external verification of whether or not a subject truly possesses Moral Nature of filial piety and fraternity.

The course of the external verification of Moral Nature is at the same time the course of the externalization of Moral Nature. If Moral Nature is genuine, then it always is not only condensed internally, but also manifests itself externally. In explaining "investigation of the world for acquirement of knowledge", Wang Yangming gave consideration at the same time to the problem of external manifestation of Moral Nature: "In my understanding of the investigation of the world for acquirement of knowledge, when I apply the innate knowledge of my Mind to everything and every object, then everything and every object all acquire its Principle." (*Records of the Instructions and Reviews*, vol.2) Everything and every object here are mainly connected with the domain of morality, for instance, the ethical relationships between men, etc. Investigation of the world and acquirement of knowledge both involve moral practice. Innate knowledge, in opposition to everything and every object, not only embodies Heavenly Principle as its substance, but also blends with "my Mind"; therefore, it can be regarded as the self-substantiated internal Moral Nature. The application of the innate knowledge of "my Mind" to everything and every object is the application of moral consciousness to moral practice (transformation of Moral Nature into moral conduct), and that everything and every object acquire its Principle implies that internal Moral Nature exhibits and reflects the ethical world. With regard to the relation between Mind and Principle, this course is demonstrated as a construction of the rationalized order of morality through the externalization of Mind; as far as the relation between Moral Nature and moral conduct is concerned, it can be regarded as an ethical relation in which Moral Nature is objectified in reality through moral conduct.

The externalization or objectification of Moral Nature is not a process far removed from daily life. The application (attainment) of innate knowledge to everything and every object already implies the relation between the externalization of Moral Nature and the world of daily life. The transformation of Moral Nature into moral conduct does not necessarily manifest a world-shaking event; on the contrary, it exists more often in minute and trivial actions. Moral relations are always unfolded in all aspects of social life, and each subject always exists in a certain set social environment, which often cannot be chosen at will. Therefore, moral practice will necessarily involve the relation between unselectivity of environment and selectivity of conduct. The strength of Moral Nature lies in that conduct is charged with new meanings through constant infiltration of daily practice in a set environment, so that the daily practice reaches the realm of the Way.

The transformation of Moral Nature into moral conduct mainly stresses the verification of Moral Nature with moral conduct. The relation between Moral Nature and moral conduct is certainly not restricted in this aspect. Moral conduct belongs to moral practice in a broad sense, and it was often categorized into the order of effort in Wang Yangming's theory, while Moral Nature with self-substantiated innate knowledge as its content was understood as noumenon. In Wang Yangming's view, there was no distinction of internality and externality of noumenon in its origin. The latter meant that noumenon manifested itself through effort, and that at the same time effort could not be separated from noumenon. In the relation between Moral Nature and moral conduct, effort in connection with noumenon means moral conduct always relies on Moral Nature as its internal basis. Different subjects have different experiences in the world of daily life, and what they do cannot be designed in detail beforehand, but no matter what differences of their actions may be, they all come out from the same self.

Moral Nature as internal noumenon usually manifests itself in the form of subjective consciousness. However, this internal conscious structure cannot be mixed with the common concept of Idea. Through distinction between innate knowledge and Idea, Wang Yangming made an explanation of it. In his view, there were different layers of meaning for the word Idea: In a broad sense, it is a synonym of Mind; but in a narrower sense, it is close to a notion. The meaning here refers to the latter. An Idea arises in reaction to an outside Matter, and has the characteristics of initiation and randomness. That an Idea arises in reaction to an outside Matter means that it comes into being because of the environment it meets and changes as the environment develops. It is completely under the sway of outside objects and lacks internal determinacy. Different from Idea, innate knowledge as true Moral Nature is not accidentally generated upon the encounter of some external environment, and it also does not exist or disappear in accordance with the existence and disappearance of its objects. It is condensed into the inner personality in the course of practice and learning; therefore, it has the quality of constancy and devotion. Because of its constancy and inner personality, inner knowledge is not changed by outside Matters and can regulate itself, evaluate itself and make judgment on the relevance of what Idea refers to.

The distinction of Idea from innate knowledge aims at the emphasis that the subject could not cling to some external encounters, but should stress the dominance of noumenon (Moral Nature) over effort (moral conduct). The world of objects is always in infinite variety and difficult to be known thoroughly, and the environments Man is in are usually changing ceaselessly. If a man follows the changing environments constantly, and is tied to some occasional words or actions in a concrete situation or environment, he usually cannot deal competently with the great variety and quantity of work, and also it is difficult for him to keep consistency of his conduct. Only when noumenon is established with Moral Nature (innate knowledge) as guidance can the subject always persevere in pursuit of goodness in different environments. Moral Nature (innate knowledge) as truthful personality manifests the internal unity of self, and in this sense, it is "the one", as in "There is only this one innate knowledge". On the other hand, moral conduct is the manifestation of the same Moral Nature in many aspects in different social relations and existing environments, so it can be regarded as "multiplicity"; thus, the dominance of Moral Nature (innate knowledge) over moral conduct can also be regarded as the dominance of one over multiplicity.

Moral conduct as the multiple manifestations of Moral Nature in concrete environments includes the actions on different occasions, and Moral Nature (innate knowledge) is the guiding principle of conduct. According to Wang Yangming, at a deeper inside level, the relation between Moral Nature (innate knowledge) and conduct is like the relation between compasses and setsquares, and circles and squares, with the former providing measurements for the latter. The restraint of Moral Nature (innate knowledge) over conduct, and noumenon over effort, is like the measuring standards of compasses and setsquares to circles and squares, with the former providing selection and regulation for the latter: It always affirms and encourages conduct appropriate to Moral Nature, and denies and rejects incompatible conduct. This kind of selection and rejection is not only corresponding to the dimension of self-evaluation embodied in innate knowledge, but also embodies the concrete presentation of the identification of emotions and the orienting function of Will. Moral Nature controls conduct in different environments right through this internal mechanism and endows unpredictable concrete conduct with internal uniformity.

In the perspective of historical development of Chinese philosophy, the early Confucian scholars already noticed the restraint of Moral Nature on conduct. Kong Zi promoted the perfection of Man (cultivation of personality) to an important position and set the realm of perfect personality as his goal in personal values. Such a personality is not only embodied in internal Moral Nature, but also externalized into the concrete course of conduct, and the latter is always regulated and guided by the former. Kong Zi said: "If a man has a will to practice benevolence, he will do nothing evil." (A Benevolent Neighborhood, *The Confucian Analects*) A will in pursuit of benevolence means pursuing and establishing the personality centered on the benevolent Way. In Kong Zi's view, if a man could do this, then he could avoid an immoral tendency (doing nothing evil) in daily conduct. On the contrary, if a man lacked such a stable personality, it was usually difficult for him to maintain his good conduct consistently. Wang Yangming demanded the restraint of noumenon on effort and the dominance of Moral Nature (innate knowledge) over concrete conduct; there is no doubt that he inherited this line of thinking. As related before, every individual is a specific historical existence, the social relationships he is in and the environments he faces are usually different, and the activities he engages in are constantly changeable and irrevocable. How can he keep consistency or conformity of conduct in different environments? It is obviously not feasible to establish strict and detailed rules and regulations for every kind of conduct. As far as the domain of morality is concerned, internal Moral Nature and personality have their functions that cannot be ignored. In contrast to the irrevocability and changeability of conduct, Moral Nature of the subject (conductor) as the self-substantiated truthful personality has its long and unbroken conformity (conformity unfolded in time). It allows the subject to maintain his moral integrity in all kinds of environments, and further diminishes the randomness of conduct. Just like Kong Zi's definition of the relation between benevolence and concrete conduct, Wang Yangming's observation about the relation between noumenon and effort, and innate knowledge and concrete conduct, seems to be derived from the above idea.

Nevertheless, in relation with the distinction between knowledge and Moral Nature, Wang Yangming could not define appropriately the position of the function of knowledge in the transformation of Moral Nature into moral conduct in his emphasis on the dominance of Moral Nature over conduct. In his view, between knowledge and internal noumenon of Mind (Moral Nature), it is important to perfect internal noumenon of Mind first. Based on this, Wang Yangming further held: "Knowledge and techniques can be left out for discussion." (*Records of the Instructions and Reviews*, vol.2) That is, in the course of the cultivation of Moral Nature, mastery of knowledge can be completely ignored, and this again goes to another extreme. Perfection of Moral Nature (noumenon of Mind) certainly is different from the acquirement of knowledge; however, the two cannot be separated. This is not only because Moral Nature itself is not restricted to knowledge, but still embodies knowledge; moreover, knowledge and techniques cannot be discarded in the transformation from Moral Nature to moral conduct. If there is only the intention of goodness without the preparation of necessary knowledge, it is easy for Moral Nature to exist as a good motive, but difficult to be transformed into reality. In this aspect, there is no doubt that Wang Yangming's understanding of the course of the transformation of Moral Nature into moral conduct had limitations in theory.

5. Distinction between Community and Self

Moral Nature as an internal quality of the subject takes self as bearer: The perfection of Moral Nature logically refers to the perfection of self. From the ethics of Moral Nature, Wang Yangming developed his theory of self-perfection. However, self is not just enclosed inside, as individual existence always implies coexistence with others. Therefore, relations grow between subjects, and between self and community. Wang Yangming introduced the theory of "oneness of all things of creation" into the domain of relations between community and self to position the relations between self and community, and between existence and co-existence. This line of thinking contains multiple theoretic meanings.

Since the pre-Qin times, the Confucian theory of study-for-self began to take form. Kong Zi already made distinction between study for self and study for others: Study for self meant self-perfection or self-realization, and study for others was to cater for others to win external praise. Denial of study for others and acceptance of study for self meant that the focus of attention was directed to perfection of self. With the development of "All hold self-cultivation as the fundament" in *The Great Learning*, the theory of self-perfection to consummation of other things in *The Doctrine of the Mean*, and the later evolution of Confucianism, much elaboration was made on the theory of study-for-self.

Wang Yangming based his theory on the perfection of Moral Nature, and naturally had a theoretic identification with the above Confucian tradition. Same as the early Confucian scholars, Wang Yangming paid great attention to the establishment of "the Mind of study-for-self", and regarded it as the starting-point of his theory. "Study-for-self" here mainly refers to self-substantiation and self-improvement. In view of the internal structure of Mindology, study-for-self can be regarded as a logic extension of the perfection of Moral Nature, and the ultimate goal is self-perfection: "A man must have the Mind of study-for-self, and he can restrain himself. Since he can restrain himself, he can then perfect himself." (*Records of the Instructions and Reviews*, vol.1, *Complete Works*, 35) Self-restraint is self-suppression. Wang Yangming regarded self-perfection as the end of the course, and self-restraint as a means of self-perfection. This means that moral cultivation is not only a self-denial; rather, it is a course of self-perfection. This affirmation of self at the same time indicates the concern for individual existence. It has in theory the internal connection with the promotion of noumenon of Mind.

The making of Will is the prerequisite for self-perfection. In Wang Yangming's theory, Will was originally the internal definition of Moral Nature. As the definition of Moral Nature, Will is different from incidental ideas, and represents a stable intention. With regards to the stable intention, Will again is connected with the goal of values (aspiration): The making of Will means self-establishment of the goal of values. In its concrete connotation, the goal of values expressed in the form of Will is nothing but sagehood, and self-perfection always directs to the attainment of sagehood. For the attainment of the realm of inner sagehood, a man must be first resolved to be a sage: "A man must make up his Mind to be a sage." (*Records of the Instructions and Reviews*, vol.3) Through establishing Will to set up the goal of values, one then can truly turn from catering to others to establishing self, and the course of study-for-self, self-restraint, and self-perfection can thus reach the internal destination.

Establishing Will to transcend secular indulgence reflects the strength of internal personality. The external form of this kind of personality is an extraordinary man. Wang Yangming recommended such extraordinary men, and held that only they could represent the independence of personality, which could retain the self's truthful Moral Nature and internal virtue, even in a time when there was little interest learning: "In addition to the hostility to learning, few people have interest in pursuit of the Way. A man in Qi State or Chu State could be quickly assimilated with local custom. If a man is not extraordinary, it is rare that he can stand on his own and does not change his Mind." (*Complete Works*, 144) That a man in Qi State or Chu State could be quickly assimilated with local custom means that a man who lived in Chu State could be assimilated with Chu custom, and if he arrived in Qi State, he could easily adapt himself to Qi habits. A man who lives in the secular world can be easily assimilated with it. Only an extraordinary man who is determined to attain sagehood can be relied on, because he refuses to submit himself to degradation and unswervingly strives for the set goal of values.

An unswerving independent extraordinary man often conducts himself in unruly manners. Therefore, he is also called "an unruly man". Wang Yangming often called himself "an unruly man". An unruly man upholds truth, has confidence in himself, keeps clear of all affectations, and is not influenced by external denouncement and honor. He not only refuses to cater for others and follow the trends, but also dares to challenge the secular views: "A great man can freely shake heaven and earth. How can he tolerate to be fettered like a desperate prisoner!" (*Complete Works*, 784) This valor of shaking heaven and earth can be regarded as a vivid description of the independent personality.

Certainly, an unruly man or an extraordinary man does not belong to the ultimate realm of personality. The ultimate goal that Will directs to is the attainment of sagehood, not becoming an unruly man. However, although the appearance and spirit of an unruly man is not the end of the course of self-perfection, it can be a logical medium to reach the realm of inner sagehood: In Wang Yangming's view, if an unruly man moved one step forward, he could enter the realm of sagehood. A man usually faces in reality the pursuit of fame and interests; however, the characteristic for an unruly man is that although he lives in the environment, he keeps himself pure with noble aspiration, remains lofty from the mundane world, and will not be assimilated with secular custom. It is in the course of rejection of and transcendence over the degradation of daily life that an unruly man advances uninterruptedly towards the realm of sagehood, as referred to in "Once he thinks of self-restraint, he is a sage right away." The above promotion of the realm of an unruly man implies at the same time the stress on the independent quality of an individual: The unrestrained independence constitutes an internal link of attaining sagehood.

The prerequisite for the transcendence over secular influence is to affirm that every man has the internal source to attain sagehood: "If you do not believe in the self-possession of the full source, please observe yourself along with development of things." (*Complete Works*, 790) This kind of self-sufficient source constitutes the internal potential of self-perfection. The realm of sagehood is not an outside imposition, and does not take form in the course of forgetting self and pursuing things either; it is more related to the development of the internal potential. Beginning from the pre-Qin times, Confucian scholars already noticed the internal basis for the perfection of manhood (perfection of ideal personality). Kong Zi put forth the theory: "Men are born with similar Nature, but their experiences differentiate them", and believed that similar Nature provided the possibility for the perfection of manhood. Meng Zi further transformed similar Nature into innate goodness of Nature, and regarded Nature of innate goodness as the starting point (beginning) to reach the realm of internal sagehood. There is no doubt that Wang Yangming's views inherited the theory of the perfection of manhood of the earliest Confucianism. If the demeanor of extraordinary men and the mettle of unruly men supported emphatically the self-establishment in the relation between individual existence and secular world, then the affirmation of self-sufficiency and self-possession of individual Nature provided further the internal basis for self-establishment.

Each person has not only the basis of attaining sagehood, but also different talent. Self-Nature as the internal basis for attaining sagehood at the same time also means that each individual must be guided and cultivated according to his own concrete characteristics. Wang Yangming generalized this Principle as: "Each man should perfect himself according to his talent." (*Records of the Instructions and Reviews*, vol.1, *Complete Works*, 21) Individual personalities are different, and methods and ways of perfecting manhood are usually various. In conformity to various ways of manhood perfection, modes of personality are also diversified. The differences in individuality make it difficult to set up a uniform mode of personality for all. If a uniform mode is imposed on all people, the individuality of Man will unavoidably be restrained or even suppressed. Obviously, Wang Yangming's emphasis on the individual talent is different from Zhu Xi's insistence on gauging men only with general Heavenly Principle.

Concreteness of personality not only unfolds itself in diversified images, but also has its internal dimension, which usually manifests itself in the form of an individual's independent thinking. As related before, in Wang Yangming's view, true Moral Nature always included the definition of self-evaluation, while self-evaluation always meant the requirement of independent thinking. When viewed in the perspective of self-perfection, having Will to attain sagehood and to transcend degradation also meant that a man was not under the sway of any external opinion or view. Wang

Yangming made the distinction between seeking answers from one's own Mind and seeking answers from outside, and held that "It is valuable in study to find answers in one's own Mind." If a man judged that a certain argument was right through his own thinking, he could not refuse it even when it came out from the mouth of a common man. (*Records of the Instructions and Reviews*, vol.2) Here it involves two ways of thinking: Blind admiration of authority and self-thinking. Between the two, the latter is undoubtedly promoted to an even more important level. Although there is no intention here to sweep away the traditional authority, it indeed reflects a pursuit of independent personality.

Of course, the self manifests more than a realm of personality, and it is always embodied in an existence of life in reality. Wang Yangming once briefly pointed out this meaning: "When has the true self ever left its body?!" (*Records of the Instructions and Reviews*, vol.1) Body is an existence of life with its perceptual physique as presentation. The true self certainly cannot be the same as the perceptual body (Wang Yangming repeatedly stressed the restraint of true self in the form of innate knowledge, etc. over body), but it is also not detached from the perceptual life. It is based on this prerequisite that Wang Yangming put forth the demand that "Do not end your life". Its intrinsic meaning should be to cherish one's own life. A man lives in the society and always faces all kinds of moral duties and obligations, but he cannot ignore the value of the individual life. The reason is that the execution of moral duties should not be directed at denying the existence of an individual life.

It seems that Wang Yangming's above view is different to some extent from the orthodox Principlism of the Chengs-Zhu School. In correspondence with the promotion of noumenon of Nature, Chengs-Zhu preferred to intensify the rationalized essence of Man. In this fixed set of thinking, the value of the existence of the individual life usually could not be put in a rational position. It is not difficult to see this point from the debate about the loss of chastity and the starvation to death: "It is extremely trivial to die of starvation, but extremely important to lose chastity." (*Collected Works of Two Chengs*, 301) As related before, the protection of chastity is in defense of Heavenly Principle (metaphysical species-essence), while life or death involves the existence of individual life. In the laws and restrictions above, in contrast to the demand of Heavenly Principle, individual existence has become totally unimportant: Behind the distinction between the extreme triviality and the extreme importance lies more than the concept of male supremacy, for the true connotation is, to some extent, the indifference for the existence of individual life. In contrast with Chengs-Zhu's stand, Wang Yangming affirmed that the true self did not leave his body, and demanded "Do not end your life", which is undoubtedly of theoretic significance in solving the tension between the Principlist essence and the existence of life.

From perfection of Moral Nature to self-perfection, the above theoretical reasoning has always been connected with the distinction between Mind-Body and noumenon of Nature. Different from noumenon of Nature which emphasizes the universal Principle, Mind-Body at the same time embodies the Principle of individuality. The latter not only embodies the inner Moral Nature of the subject, but also presents "I" as a concrete existence. In view of noumenon of Nature, the focus of attention primarily goes to species-essence and universal norm, while the focus based on Mind-Body will hardly neglect individual existence. As far as this point is concerned, Wang Yangming's theory of self-perfection can also be regarded as the logic unfoldment of his Mindology.

Self-perfection as the goal of values does not mean a lead to self-centeredness. As mentioned previously, Wang Yangming held that the connotations of self-perfection and attainment of sagehood were conformable, and the internal sagehood always refused self-enclosure. In the internal logic of Wang Yangming's theory, Mind-Body as the basis of self-perfection contains both the definition of individuality and the dimension of universality, and the latter also restrains the theoretical orientation of self-perfection. As a matter of fact, when Wang Yangming affirmed study-for-self and rejected study-for-others, what he rejected was self-degradation in morality, not the co-existence of self and others. As the concrete form of Moral Nature, self is at the same time manifested as an open subject.

Oneness of all things of creation is a basic belief of Wang Yangming. In his writings, we can see repeatedly such remarks. "The benevolent man is in oneness with heaven, earth, and all things of creation." (*Records of the Instructions and Reviews*, vol.1) As a philosophical proposition with extensive coverage, oneness of all things of creation means the unity of Man and Nature. In terms of the relation between self and community, oneness of all things of creation takes as its connotation the mutual connection between different subjects. Of course the concept of oneness of all things of creation was not first put forth by Wang Yangming, as Zhang Zai, Chengs-Zhu, etc., already had the similar views. However, Wang Yangming further understood it as a Principle of communication between subjects.

An individual as a social existence always shares social spaces with others, and forms a relation of coexistence. This coexistence unfolds itself firstly in the world of daily life (conventional life and practice) that undoubtedly has its side of secularity. Therefore, it is unavoidable that the identification with nothing but the world of daily life leads easily to secularization. Obviously, Wang Yangming had the intention of transcending secularization in demanding self-establishment through making Will to attain sagehood. However, if the coexistence per se, because of its secular dimension of the world of daily life, is considered as degradation, it usually leads to self-enclosure. In the modern existentialism, it is not difficult for us to see such a tendency. Existentialism certainly noticed the ontological fact of the coexistence of self and others, but it regarded the self in coexistence as a degraded self, and thought that the internal experiences of boredom, fear, anxiety, etc. were the way of the existence of the true self. This view in fact guided the transcendence over secularity to the escape from coexistence. As far as the coexistence between self and others is concerned, self-establishment in the transcendence over secularity mainly manifests a self-orientation in a negative aspect. In fact, this kind of transcendence does not adopt the way of the escape from coexistence, and its real sense lies in the attainment of the sublime and brilliant realm by following the doctrine of the mean. In the positive aspect, the self again should face others with magnanimity, and express sincere concern, friendship and love so that the relation between subjects assume the meaning of the Way of benevolence. In highly recommending the remarkable self-established valor of unruly men, Wang Yangming at the same time regarded the benevolent spirit of oneness of all things of creation as the Principle of communication between subjects, which undoubtedly indicates the tendency of uniting the two above aspects.

How to construct a rational relation between subjects is a problem that both Chinese and Western philosophers showed their interest in a long time ago. Relatively speaking, the Western philosophers focused more on the principle of justice. According to Aristotle, justice meant every individual could obtain what he deserved. In the positive respect, obtaining what one deserves means fulfilling the rights that he possesses as an individual, and its core is the universal respect and affirmation of rights. This principle in the relation between subjects not only demonstrates each subject's affirmation of his own rights, but also shows the mutual respect for the reciprocal rights of the two sides in communication. The principle of justice always involves the just allocation of interests, and is correspondingly related to the benefits in real life. From ancient Greece to the modern times, the Western philosophy has always paid ample attention to the principle of justice. Indeed, this principle is indispensible in constructing the rational relation between subjects, but if the individual rights and the relevant interests are over-intensified, it is also easy to cause alienation between members of the community, and even conflicts. Wang Yangming also noticed the malpractice of excessive concern about personal interests, and regarded the persistent coveting of personal interests as the causes of separation between people and mutual harm between close relatives. This view may be seen as treating the individual rights with indifference, but at the same time it points out the negative consequences in the kind of communication that is based on an exchange of interests.

In contrast with this exchange of interests, Wang Yangming emphasized the emotional exchange between subjects. In his view, Man as the soul of heaven and earth (the spirit of all things of creation) should possess universal benevolence and sympathy. This sympathy could enable Man to transcend the distinction between self and others, and achieve the unity between subjects. In this sense, benevolence and sympathy constituted a psychological and emotional basis for the connection between subjects. He firmly believed that if every individual could apply benevolence and sympathy to all people in the world, from self to others, from near to far, then the ideal of oneness of all things of creation could gradually be realized.

There is no doubt that Wang Yangming was too optimistic and even simplified the problem when he regarded compassion as a guarantee for oneness of all things of creation and held that the extensive promotion of benevolence and sympathy could dissolve the isolation among people. The relationship between subjects involves not only psychological emotions, but also in a broad sense, the related social structure, system, formalized procedures in their communication, etc. Nevertheless, what Wang Yangming said above has a point worth noting: When he interpreted benevolence and sympathy as the psychological and emotional basis for communication between subjects, his internal intention was to demand the Way of benevolence be accepted as the principle for exchange between subjects. At a general theoretic level, the key of this principle is to respect and affirm the internal value of every subject. It not only affirms the will of self-realization of the subject, but also demands the sincere acceptance of the significance of mutual existence between subjects. Kong Zi defined benevolence as love of people, and Meng Zi held compassion as the beginning of benevolence, etc.; they both expressed the emphasis on the internal value of every subject. Here it not only embodies the rational prerequisite of Man as purpose, but also is filled with emotional identification between subjects. Exchange between subjects of course cannot be conducted without dialogues in language, but with communication in language only; there is no more than knowing the meaning and understanding each other, whereas the emotional identification based on the Way of benevolence can often enable people to further grasp the implications and achieve mutual understanding. In a word, the Principle of the Way of benevolence demands that the subject care about the significance of self-existence, and go out of self-enclosure to communicate with others through the mutual affirmation of the value of the existence between self and others. Wang Yangming regarded benevolence and sympathy as the internal guarantee for the realization of oneness of all things of creation. It certainly had its abstract aspect, but at the same time it seemed to more or less reflect the function of the norms of the Principle of the Way of benevolence in the communication between subjects. Undoubtedly it has great theoretical significance in restraining the tendency of communication based on an exchange of interests.

The Principle of the Way of benevolence in the communication with others requires the mutual respect between subjects. In the third volume of *Records of the Instructions and Reviews*, there is one thought-provoking dialogue between Wang Yangming and his disciple. One day, the disciple returned from an outing and said to Wang Yangming: "I've found an unusual thing today." "What's unusual?" Wang Yangming asked. The disciple replied: "I saw the street was crowded with sages." Then Wang Yangming remarked: "It is quite usual. Why do you feel surprised?" At first look, such question and answer are close to the sharp-witted and incisive remarks of the Chan sect, but in fact they have an implied message. That the street is crowded with sages doesn't mean whoever one meets in the street has attained the ideal realm of personality. The implied message is that every subject in a social community deserves respect. Logically speaking, since the street is crowded with sages, then one cannot have a feeling of moral supremacy in the course of communication or treat others condescendingly. He said: "Suppose you invite a sage to give a lecture. When people see a sage coming, they are so awed as to leave in a hurry. How can he give his lecture?" (*Ibid.*) The departure because of awe indicates a psychological distance that leads to the separation between self and others. Only by treating all people like sages and treating others with such an equal attitude can the psychological distance be dissolved to achieve mutual understanding.

With oneness of all things of creation as the general guideline, Wang

Yangming defined in multiple aspects the relations between self and community, and between subjects. His emphasis was to overcome the separation between self and others, and to work towards an understanding between subjects. The discussion of the relation between subjects in the form of oneness of all things of creation is naturally in a somewhat speculative vein, but in view of the internal structure of Wang Yangming's philosophy, it is an indispensable aspect of the system. As related before, Wang Yangming established his theory on the basis of Mind-Body, constructed the world of meaning with Mind, and transformed it concretely into Moral Nature to guide conduct. The promotion of Mind-Body in combination with the theory of study-for-self logically embodies the possibility that leads to the over-intensification of the individual principle, and this trend can be curbed effectively with the theory of oneness of all things of creation. Of course, although the theory of the relation between subjects unfolded from the theory of oneness of all things of creation involves how to dissolve the tension between self and others, and makes some valuable study about the principle of reasonable communication, it also demonstrates the tendency of excessive restriction of the relation between self and others in the holistic dimension, which in theory will potentially lead to the theory of non-self.

The relation between self and community is repeatedly analyzed by Confucian scholars. In the pre-Qin times, the early Confucian scholars already paid attention to this issue. Kong Zi put forth the theory of "self-cultivation for stability of others". Self-cultivation is to perfect self, and "stability of others" points to social community (realization of collective value). Stability of others as the purpose of self-perfection embodies the identification with community and the emphasis on individual social responsibility. *The Great Learning* as one of the Confucian classics follows this line of thought, and formulated even more specific definitions on the relation between cultivation, regulation, governance, and pacification: "When a man is well-cultivated, he regulates his family; when his family is well-regulated, he then governs the country; when the country is well-governed, then the whole world becomes pacified." Here the starting point is self-perfection, and the purpose of the whole course is the realization of collective value — when the country is well-governed, the whole world becomes pacified. The latter constitutes the social responsibility that an individual should bear. With the development of Confucianism, emphasis on community identity gradually became a fixed pattern of Confucian thought. In what Wang Yangming expounded above, we can see the influence of this same pattern of thought. In view of the relation between self and community, affirming the social responsibility that an individual should bear and demanding the identification with community value doubtlessly help to restrict and avoid the tendency of self-centeredness. Wang Yangming once criticized that the Buddhist Chan sect kept outside of ethical relations and ignored the worldly affairs (escaping from social responsibility). Its significance is obviously not restricted in the dispute between Confucianism and Buddhism (negation of the Buddhist negligence of self's social obligations with the Confucian principle of community): In an even broader sense, it can be regarded as rejection of the principle of self-centered value.

However, because of the criticism that the Buddhist Chan sect kept outside of ethical relations, Wang Yangming unavoidably over-intensified the social responsibility of an individual. In talking about the relations between monarch and subjects, and self and country, Wang Yangming already expressed clearly such a tendency: "When a subject serves his monarch, he is willing to kill himself if it benefits the country, and to sacrifice his clan if it can bring advantage to the monarch. How can the personal fortune and trivial fame interrupt his aspiration!" (*Complete Works*, 474) The "country" here can be regarded as the symbol of the entire social community, and the monarch is the epitome of this entirety. Here the relation of self and community is unfolded as the relation between individual and collective, while the social responsibility of individuals can be demonstrated as absolute submission of the self to the collective: For "the benefits of the country" and "the advantages to the monarch", the self must give up all unconditionally; even with dedication of life and sacrifice of his clan, he should have no regret. It is not difficult to see that in this relation, the collective seems to take an abstract form: It is united with the monarch and transcends the individual, while the self as individual is submerged in the universal social obligations.

In conformity with the transcendental collective transformed abstractly from community and the demand of absolute submission of individual to collective, Wang Yangming put forward the theory of non-self: "The sage based his philosophy on non-self, and attained it with valor." (*Complete Works*, 232) In the aspect of study-for-self, non-self stresses that one should not be restricted to one's own view. The non-self in this sense is close to what Kong Zi advocated: "No conjecture, no arbitrariness, no obstinacy, no egoism." (*The Confucian Analects*) As for the relations between self and community, and self and others, non-self demands a self that is open instead of closed, and tries to cover self identity with community identity. This of course does not mean giving up self-realization, for in relation to the intensification of community identity, self-perfection is not isolated from non-self: "The study of superior men is that of self-perfection. It is because of self-perfection that one must restrain himself, and self-restraint leads to non-self. Non-self means non-I." (*Complete Works*, 272) While defining non-self as a meaning in the topic of study-for-self certainly avoids understanding self-perfection as self-centeredness, this connection between self-realization and non-self may lead to the possibility that the concretely defined substance of self is lost: The "I" attained through self-restraint and non-self may have a weakened character in reality.

The connection between subjects cannot be separated from any concrete and real individual. Only in the social connection can the essence of Man be realized in its concrete presentation, but this kind of connection itself must be realized in concrete individuals. Although Wang Yangming transformed transcendental Heavenly Principle with innate knowledge, and at the same time affirmed the individual quality of the self, he more or less abstracted self and community unavoidably when he defined them at the level of social relationship: In the premise of non-self, the community becomes somewhat a general transcendental power over the individual, and it seems difficult for the individual per se to realize his concrete existence.

As mentioned previously, the establishment of Mind-Body means the abandonment of the external imposition of the transcendental Principle over the individual, but it also provides a possibility for the one-sided inflation of individuality. From the transformation of innate knowledge into Moral Nature, to the theory of study-for-self and the theory of self-perfection, the aspect of individuality is mainly unfolded; on the other hand, the theory of oneness of all things of creation through the transformation from subjects to inter-subjects restricts the evolution from self-perfection to self-centeredness. The latter at the same time inherits the traditional distinction between self and community. The theory of oneness of all things of creation in combination with the tradition of distinction between Confucianism and Buddhism, and the Confucian solicitude of community promotes the community principle that emphasizes social responsibilities of the individual, which further leads to the theory of non-self. The above course of Wang Yangming's thinking manifests not only its own internal logical connection, but also an unsolved difficult theoretical problem to the speculative Mindology in the rational positioning of the relations between self and others, and self and community.

6. To Attain Innate Knowledge

Wang Yangming once drew a conclusion: "What I have lectured in my life is nothing but three words — 'attain innate knowledge'." To attain innate knowledge is an important topic in his Mindology, and its origin can be traced back to *The Great Learning*. The theory of rectification of Mind, sincerity of intention, investigation of things, and attainment of knowledge in *The Great Learning* had undoubtedly influenced Wang Yangming's proposition of attainment of innate knowledge. Certainly, Wang Yangming had his own definition about "attainment". In his view on the whole, there was a dual meaning for the word. The first was "to reach", that is, to arrive at. It did not mean any increase of experiential knowledge, but the attainment of the goal of the self-consciousness of internal innate knowledge (details in the later explanation). Another meaning of attainment was "to do" or to practice. Wang Yangming himself had an even clearer generalization about it: "To be resolved to put it in practice is to attain innate knowledge." (*Complete Works*, 277) This meaning of attaining innate knowledge has already combined with the distinction between knowledge and action, and its theoretic meaning will be further discussed in detail in the distinction between knowledge and action.

Wang Yangming held that there was a possibility for every individual to attain sagehood, and the realization of this possibility must attain the self-consciousness of innate knowledge. So he made a distinction between the original state and the apperceptive state of innate knowledge. The former had the original attribute, and the latter was the self-consciousness of innate knowledge. When innate knowledge in relation to its subject was still in the original state, the subject usually manifested himself in an original existence; in order to reach the apperceptive state from the original state, "attainment" served as a medium.

As mentioned above, innate knowledge, as the internal moral consciousness and the fundamentals of Principlism, possesses the attribute of apriority. This apriority is first related to its origin: The formation of innate knowledge precedes any experiential activity. But this a priori formation does not necessarily mean a priori attainment of apperception. Innate knowledge as the fundamentals of Principlism is certainly a priori (in Wang Yangming's view, it was this apriority that determined its universality), and its function cannot be completely separated from a posteriori activity of the attainment of innate knowledge. It is in this sense that Wang Yangming believed: "Who does not have this innate knowledge? Only some cannot attain it." (*Complete Works*, 279) He repeatedly criticized that his contemporaries made light of the word "attainment". Such a stress on the word holds logically the distinction between a priori principle and a posteriori apperception as the prerequisite.

It can be seen that according to Wang Yangming's understanding, apriority of innate knowledge certainly guaranteed universal effectiveness of innate knowledge, but it could not guarantee the subject's self-consciousness of innate knowledge. This distinction between apriority and apperception doubtlessly has theoretic significance. Logically speaking, a priori completion usually means certain restrictions on the function of the subject: As the bestowal of heaven, the formation of innate knowledge is not the result of the subject's study and thinking. However, if a priori knowledge at first only possesses the original attribute, only through the course of the attainment of innate knowledge can apperceptive knowledge be elevated; then, the subject's study and thinking become a necessary step that cannot be skipped. It is based on this prerequisite that Wang Yangming made a somewhat epistemological study of the course of the attainment of innate knowledge.

Although innate knowledge possesses a priori attribute, the attainment of innate knowledge as a course cannot be separated completely from a posteriori experiential activity and rational activity. As to the relation between innate knowledge and experience, only through imperceptible influence in daily life can the subject gradually have a feeling of identification with innate knowledge and have an intimate understanding of innate knowledge. In the same way, rational thinking is an indispensible link in the experiential understanding of innate knowledge: Only through profound thinking can the understanding of innate knowledge be led from a vague and shallow state to clarity and depth: "All possible thinking aims only at the attainment of innate knowledge. The more one thinks about innate knowledge, the more profound and clearer it becomes. Without profound thinking, a man deals with things carelessly as they take place, and innate knowledge will be crude." (*Records of the Instructions and Reviews*, vol.3) However, in Wang Yangming's view, experience and rationality was certainly indispensible in the self-conscious command of a priori noumenon, but their activity per se again could not be separated from innate knowledge. In view of the course, innate knowledge attained in a certain phase (self-conscious understanding in experience) constitutes in turn the prerequisite for further experience.

According to Wang Yangming's understanding, innate knowledge usually applied uniformity to the course of attaining innate knowledge. This function Wang Yangming called "dominant oneness". This dominant oneness is not indulgence in certain individual preference, but always takes the fundamentals of Principlism embedded in innate knowledge as the goal of pursuit, and at the same time puts all the aspects of the activity of attaining innate knowledge under this general goal. In essence, innate knowledge as the fixed goal of the course of attaining innate knowledge defines and guides the whole course. It is this goal that connects all the concrete links in different branches and phases of the course of attaining innate knowledge. In Wang Yangming's view, without the function of regulation and guidance of this a priori knowledge, it would be inevitable that all would fall into a state of "discreteness". The discreteness here means different activities remain at different links of branches and phases, and cannot be synthesized together to form a unified moral consciousness. Here, the "innate knowledge of my Mind" becomes the logical prerequisite of the possible unified moral concept.

In the above unfoldment of the course of attaining innate knowledge, on the one hand, only through this course of attaining innate knowledge can the subject self-consciously have a command of a priori innate knowledge, and on the other hand, the course of attaining innate knowledge per se is constrained by innate knowledge. "Knowledge" and "attainment" are in interaction, become mutually prerequisites, and manifest a unified dynamic relation. It is in this reciprocal course from innate knowledge to the attainment of innate knowledge, and from the attainment of innate knowledge to innate knowledge, that a priori innate knowledge is gradually transformed from the original state to the apperceptive knowledge.

In an overall view, on the side of "attainment" (arrival, realization), the attainment of innate knowledge not only manifests the transformation from a priori moral noumenon into Moral Nature in reality, but also means the transformation of the original innate knowledge into the apperceptive knowledge (constant attainment of self-consciousness of innate knowledge). Innate knowledge is bestowed by heaven but exists inside human mind, but if it only remains in this original state, then "Although it is called innate knowledge, still it is not known as innate knowledge."

(*Questions on The Great Learning*) Only through the course of "attainment" can it be really self-substantiated. Wang Yangming's above definition of the relation between innate knowledge and the attainment of innate knowledge indicates his thought of the unity of a priori innate knowledge and a posteriori attainment of innate knowledge. In the development of Confucianism, this unity of innate knowledge and the attainment of innate knowledge can be regarded as a blend of Meng Zi's theory of innate knowledge and the theory of the attainment of innate knowledge in *The Great Learning*. In the perspective of the internal structure of Mindology, it again constitutes the logical prerequisite of the theory of noumenon and effort.

In Wang Yangming's theory, innate knowledge right at the beginning assumed the meaning of spiritual noumenon, and the attainment of innate knowledge was manifested as a posteriori effort. The relation between innate knowledge and the attainment of innate knowledge was logically unfolded as the distinction between noumenon and effort. In correspondence with the thought of the unity of innate knowledge and attainment of innate knowledge, Wang Yangming paid much attention to the unity of noumenon and effort.

As for the relation between noumenon and effort, Wang Yangming provided specific definitions in two aspects, i.e. the interpretation of effort from the aspect of noumenon, and the interpretation of noumenon from the aspect of effort. The former emphasized the restraint of noumenon on effort, and the latter stressed that only in the course of unfoldment of effort can noumenon obtain its quality in reality. In terms of their contents, noumenon manifests a comprehensive unity of consciousness, and effort is a posteriori course of cognition and practice. As far as his affirmation of apriority of noumenon is concerned, Wang Yangming's way of thinking obviously did not break through the domain of speculative philosophy. However, as he emphasized that only in the course of unfoldment of effort could noumenon obtain the real quality and be understood self-consciously by the subject, there was also the aspect of the sublation of the transcendence of noumenon. In the development of philosophy, when Zhu Xi bestowed noumenon of Nature with apriority, again he stressed the aspect of the transcendence of noumenon of Nature over Mind of Man at the experiential level. This view in logic embodied the unity of apriority and transcendence: Noumenon is not only a priori, but also transcendental. As the unity of apriority and transcendence, noumenon possesses predominantly the metaphysical arbitrariness. Wang Yangming's dual interpretation of effort from the aspect of noumenon and of noumenon from the aspect of effort, to some extent, made a distinction between apriority and transcendence; therefore, it provided the theoretic prerequisite for the restoration from the noumenon of consciousness to the cognitive process in reality.

Cognitive activity in a broad sense is always unfolded as a course of constant transformation of the objective world (including the natural world) into the world of meaning. The course in which the subject gives meaning to the objects cannot be separated from the internal conscious structure (spiritual noumenon): The degree of understanding the objects is connected with the level that the internal spiritual noumenon (conscious structure) can reach. As to this point, the spiritual noumenon can be regarded as the internal basis of spiritual activity (the course of giving meaning). However, the spiritual noumenon per se is not a transcendental existence, but is always in a historical course: It in essence takes form in man's historical practice and spiritual activity, and is constantly enriched with contents in the development of the course. Historicity of spiritual noumenon and historicity of spiritual activity can be regarded as the two aspects of the same course.

However, it seems that Wang Yangming had not really understood in his Mindology the above relation between spiritual noumenon and spiritual activity. Through the affirmation of "interpretation of effort from the aspect of noumenon", Wang Yangming certainly saw the function of spiritual noumenon in the transformation of the original world into the world of meaning, but this function of noumenon in Mindology again is based on its apriority. This "foresight" logically restricted Wang Yangming's understanding of "interpretation of noumenon from the aspect of effort".

If the way of thinking in interpretation of noumenon from the aspect of effort is carried out to the end, we should admit that noumenon per se is in the historical course of spiritual activity. However, in the Mindological system, the function of effort (spiritual activity) is mainly attributed to the self-conscious understanding of a priori noumenon, while noumenon that effort directs to is regarded as a priori consummate and established existence. This view obviously fails to recognize the historicity of spiritual noumenon per se. The theoretical inconformity between historicity of effort and non-historicity of noumenon manifests the internal tension of Mindology in one aspect.

7.   Unity of Knowledge and Action

In connection with the theory of the attainment of innate knowledge is the distinction between knowledge and action. Although it is very difficult to mark out strictly the time sequence between the theory of knowledge and action, and the doctrine of the attainment of innate knowledge, in the perspective of the internal structure of Mindology, the theory of knowledge and action can be regarded as the logical unfoldment of the theory of the attainment of innate knowledge. Huang Zongxi once said: In Wang Yangming's theory of attainment of innate knowledge, "Attainment is action." This view noticed that both the theory of the attainment of innate knowledge and the theory of knowledge and action had their respective theoretical emphases.

As the unfoldment of the theory of the attainment of innate knowledge, the theory of knowledge and action regarded how to attain innate knowledge as a part of its topic. As mentioned above, "to attain" has dual connotation: attainment and action. According to Wang Yangming's understanding, innate knowledge as noumenon had its apriority, but at the same time, he also made the distinction between the original state and the apperceptive state of innate knowledge: Although every subject was certainly endowed with innate knowledge, it at first was only an original (natural) knowledge; the goal of the attainment of innate knowledge was to transform the natural state into the apperceptive state, while the course of action was an inalienable part in realizing this transformation. Here action becomes the primary condition for the attainment of apperceptive knowledge.

In terms of the relation between the subject and innate knowledge, innate knowledge is of course a priori noumenon, but in a priori form, it is chiefly manifested as a logical universal and necessary knowledge, and has not been transformed into a rational consciousness in reality. Apriority provides a kind of "guarantee" for universal necessity, but before it is actually attained, innate knowledge lacks the quality of reality. Only through the course of earnest practice can the subject gradually obtain the sense of identity with and closeness to innate knowledge, and transform it into rational consciousness of his own accord. It is in this sense that Wang Yangming repeatedly emphasized: "Without action, it cannot be called 'attaining innate knowledge'." (*Records of the Instructions and Reviews*, vol. 2) Here, the course of the attainment of innate knowledge has already been understood as the unity of knowledge and action, and its content is represented as that a priori innate knowledge through action (actual attainment) is transformed from the original state into the apperceptive state.

The generalization of the relation between knowledge and action as the unity of knowledge and action constitutes the unique characteristic of Wang Yangming's theory of knowledge and action. The unity of knowledge and action has multiple connotations, and Wang Yangming's expositions and definitions are usually unfolded in different aspects. In terms of the attainment of innate knowledge (arriving at or obtaining innate knowledge), the unity of knowledge and action did not present a static identity, but was unfolded as a dynamic course of transformation: It starts from presupposed innate knowledge, through a posteriori actual practice (action), and finally attains apperceptive innate knowledge. The innate knowledge as the starting point possesses a priori universal necessity, but it has not obtained the real form of rational consciousness; the apperceptive knowledge as the end certainly takes innate knowledge as its content, but this innate knowledge has abandoned its original state and obtained a conscious quality. The above course of the unity of knowledge and action can be briefly generalized as: knowledge (original state of innate knowledge) — action (actual practice) — knowledge (apperceptive innate knowledge).

Action (practical effort) is an experiential activity. Innate knowledge is a priori noumenon; its attainment of self-consciousness of a priori noumenon through a posteriori practice doubtlessly involves the relation between a priori innate knowledge and experiential activity. In the analysis of noumenon and effort, Wang Yangming characterized noumenon with apriority, and at the same time he again emphasized that only through a posteriori efforts could noumenon obtain its quality in reality. The distinction between knowledge and action can be regarded as the extension of this line of thought. Of course, different from a general experiential activity, action (practice) is a course of "doing in body and mind", for it focuses on self-substantiation. Wang Yangming held a posteriori experiential activity (action) as the prerequisite of the attainment of a priori innate noumenon, and expressed an intention of connecting transcendence and experience in the relation between knowledge and action. In terms of the original state of the theory, transcendence and experience seem difficult to come together: Transcendental presupposition is a speculative fabrication, and its purport is to provide certain metaphysical basis for the universal necessity of Principlist noumenon. Practice (action) as experiential activity directs to the relation between subject and object and the relation between subjects, while in the theory of the unity of knowledge and action, the two are mixed into one. This tendency manifests from one aspect Wang Yangming's wavering to some extent between the speculative stand and the realistic dimension: On the one hand, it has always been difficult for him to give up a priori commitment to the universal necessity of Principlist noumenon; on the other hand, he strived to allow this noumenon to abandon its transcendental attribute in the social ethical relationships and gain some strength in reality.

The unity of knowledge and action as a course consists of knowledge (original innate knowledge) — action (practice) — knowledge (apperceptive innate knowledge) as its contents. In the aspect of the attainment of innate knowledge (arrival at the self-consciousness of innate knowledge), the importance is firstly laid on the last two links (action — apperceptive innate knowledge) in the general course of innate knowledge — action — apperceptive innate knowledge. Wang Yangming emphasized that without action, one could not study for self. His implied meaning was to include action into the course of the attainment of innate knowledge. In verifying that the obtainment of knowledge (or the self-consciousness of innate knowledge) was inseparable from action, Wang Yanming often drew support from daily experiential facts, such as: To know the taste of food, one must taste it himself; to know whether the road is smooth, one should walk on it himself. (*Records of the Instructions and Review*, vol.2) Strictly speaking, the taste of food and the smoothness of a road are knowledge in the experiential domain, and their obtainment through action is not sufficient to prove that a priori noumenon (innate knowledge) can also attain self-consciousness through experiential activity. However, from a different aspect, it seems that Wang Yangming went beyond the domain of the attainment of innate knowledge to touch upon cognitive activity in a general sense, and also paid attention to the dependence of knowledge on action in this domain.

Action as a link in the course of attaining innate knowledge also constitutes the criterion for the judgment of true knowledge. The central argument here is still the inseparability between knowledge and action. Nevertheless, the emphasis here is judging innate knowledge with action: "Innate knowledge without action is still knowledge unknown." (*Records of the Instructions and Reviews*, vol.1) That is, only the knowledge obtained through action is true knowledge. This aspect of the relation between knowledge and action unfolds another connotation of the distinction between knowledge and action: Knowledge should be applied to action. According to Wang Yangming's understanding, true knowledge always included a factor of application in action, and only when it was applied to action could knowledge be realized in reality. In this sense, action is not only the medium of the attainment (understanding) of knowledge, but also constitutes the concrete way of the existence of knowledge. The unity of knowledge and action at the same time contains the dual connotation.

In Wang Yangming's theory, the course of attaining innate knowledge was not about the accumulation of knowledge, but was directed towards self-realization as stressed in "After the attainment of innate knowledge, self-intention can be realized." (*Records of the Instructions and Reviews*, vol.2) Self-realization took the perfection of Moral Nature as its concrete content, and Wang Yangming demanded "constant effort in the practice on things". This kind of effort is also regarded as the way of self-cultivation of Moral Nature, and the above unity between Moral Nature and effort then constitutes one of the connotations of the unity of knowledge and action. In the perspective of the perfection of Moral Nature, the unity of knowledge and action at the same time means the unity of the cultivation of Moral Nature and the moral practice. As related previously, in Wang Yangming's view, every man had his a priori noumenon, which constituted the internal basis of Moral Nature. However, the subject in a posteriori environment was usually influenced by secular customs to develop a "habitual Mind"; therefore, it was unavoidable for him to deviate from innate noumenon. One of the purports of going from action to the attainment of innate knowledge was to eliminate the "habitual Mind" and return to the noumenon of perfect goodness. This course of eliminating the habitual Mind did not present itself as a groundless meditation of noumenon, but unfolded itself in the moral practice of daily routine. Only through interaction between knowledge and action could a priori noumenon be transformed from the natural state into the apperceptive state, and accordingly, only in the actual effort of experiential action could the basis of perfect goodness be transformed into Moral Nature in reality.

It seems that Wang Yangming's above view is different from Zhu Xi's theory of moral self-restraint. Zhu Xi regarded the experiential identification of Heavenly Principle as the top priority of the cultivation of Moral Nature, and correspondingly connected moral self-restraint with "observance in reverence and exhaustive investigation of Principle". The latter is foremostly a state of introspective view of the subject, and its characteristics were awe, discretion, and self-restraint in spirit. Although Zhu Xi did not completely deny the relation between self-restraint and practice, relatively speaking, he emphasized the dimension of Principlist self-consciousness in the cultivation of Moral Nature (which is called "exhaustive investigation of Heavenly Principle and clear distinction of ethical relationships"), and as to the significance of moral practice in the course of the perfection of Moral Nature, he could not put it in an appropriate position. Generally speaking, the cultivation of Moral Nature is certainly related to moral knowledge through the exhaustive study of Principle, but more importantly it needs the self-chastening in the trials and tribulations of the real life of moral practice. Morality in essence is practical, moral knowledge per se takes form in moral practice, and only in the moral practice can moral ideal be transformed into reality. If a man is blinded by metaphysical thinking in emptiness and quietude without moral practice in reality, it will be very difficult for Moral Nature to obtain self-substantiated quality. Wang Yangming demanded the perfection of Moral Nature through experiential enlightenment and practice of daily routine. There is no doubt that he consciously noticed the function of moral practice in the cultivation of Moral Nature.

It can be seen that the interaction between knowledge and action, and the perfection of Moral Nature constitute the two aspects of the same course. Wang Yangming thus drew the following generalization about it: "I myself only focus on the exposition of the attainment of innate knowledge. To attain innate knowledge on things at any time is to investigate things, and to attain innate knowledge earnestly is thus self-realization." (*Records of the Instructions and Reviews*, vol.2) Going from the investigation of things to the attainment of innate knowledge depends on the self-consciousness of a priori innate knowledge, and self-realization directs to the perfection of Moral Nature. Here the transformation of original innate knowledge into apperceptive innate knowledge and the cultivation of Moral Nature are united in actual effort (action) based "on things". Wang Yangming's above thought can be regarded as a further elaboration of the Confucian theory of the unity of benevolence and knowledge in the pre-Qin times, and it more or less noticed that Principlist self-consciousness, sublimation of Moral Nature, and a posteriori actual practice are a unified course.

The formation of Moral Nature is associated with its performance. The unity of knowledge and action means not only the perfection of Moral Nature in practice, but also aims at the transformation of Moral Nature into moral practice. Wang Yangming took filial piety as an example, and said: In terms of filial piety and fraternity, undoubtedly they were good qualities but only remained at the level of concept, and could not reflect real Moral Nature of filial piety and fraternity. Only in the action of filial piety and fraternity could filial and fraternal qualities be demonstrated. (*Records of the Instructions and Reviews*, vol.1) Here the knowledge of filial piety and fraternity refers not only to the understanding of their connotations, but also to the identification and acceptance of filial piety and fraternity (internalization of them as Moral Nature). In regard to the former, whether the connotations of filial piety and fraternity are understood can be judged only through the application of action; and as to the latter, the identification and acceptance of the qualities of filial piety and fraternity must be verified through the moral action of filial piety and fraternity. The inseparability of knowledge and action is here manifested concretely as the unity of Moral Nature and moral action.

In the general order of knowledge-action-knowledge, Wang Yangming interpreted the relation between knowledge and action as a double transformative course from knowledge (original innate knowledge) to action, and from action to knowledge (apperceptive innate knowledge), and this course at the same time manifests a unity of Moral Nature and moral action. This understanding of the relation between knowledge and action is different from the abstract affirmation of the unity of knowledge and action, and involves the real movement of knowledge and action through the introduction of a course. Before Wang Yangming, Zhu Xi once put forth his theory of "knowledge first and action second". Although Zhu Xi did not deny the relation between knowledge and action, usually this kind of relation stressed the following dual meaning: First, knowledge should be applied to action; second, action should follow knowledge. In these two situations, the two courses of knowing were completed before action. Talking about the formation and attainment of innate knowledge without action often leads to a split of knowledge and action (formation of knowledge as one part, action of knowledge as another) and their abstraction. In contrast, Wang Yangming interpreted the relation between knowledge and action with the theory of interaction and transformation between knowledge and action. It seems that he linked and connected knowledge and action in the standpoint of a course.

Of course, while affirming the unity of knowledge and action, Wang Yangming also showed a tendency to obscure the distinction between knowledge and action. For instance, in order to completely eliminate unwanted motive at the conceptual level, Wang Yangming emphasized "Once an idea initiates, it is action." (*Records of the Instructions and Reviews*, vol.3) Here the so-called idea is a motive at the conceptual level. When an idea initiates, i.e. a motive is formed at the conceptual level of concept, the motive is still in the domain of consciousness, and has not been transformed into action. Logically speaking, here lies the confusion of the conceptual connotations. In terms of the relation between knowledge and action, a tendency of regarding knowledge as action is apparent. In view of this aspect, as Wang Fuzhi justly criticized later, Wang Yangming's theory of knowledge and action certainly includes regarding knowledge as action.

Chapter Three

Mindology and Thoughts in the Late Ming Dynasty

Wang Yangming's Mindology, once coming into existence, began to exert increasingly extensive influence. According to *Chronological Biography of Wang Yangming*, in his late years, the people attending his lectures were so many that the number often reached several hundred. Visiting students could not find any accommodation and had to resort to neighbouring monasteries, where one room was usually crowded with dozens of people, and their sounds of reading and reciting, singing and playing music instruments could be heard in mornings and evenings. Such was the popularity of his lectures at the time. The education of academies was popular during the Song and Ming Dynasties, but it seems hard to find such a record of popularity for any other private institutions. Therefore, it is not difficult to imagine the extensive influence of Wang Yangming's Mindology at that time. This influence of course was not limited to Wang Yangming's lifetime; in fact, Mindology after the middle of the Ming Dynasty soon became a prevailing trend of thought and developed in diversified orientations.

In his *Academic Cases of the Confucian Scholars in the Ming Dynasty*, Huang Zongxi divided the Wang Yangming school into six subdivisions according to the geographical distribution of his disciples, i.e. Mid-Zhejiang Sect, West of the Yangtze River Sect, Middle South Sect, Mid-Chu Sect, North Sect, and Guangdong and Fujian Sect. Nevertheless, this division was only based on the geographical distribution of Wang

Yangming's disciples, not on the differences of their thoughts. In terms of the lineage in the development of Mindology, attention should be paid to different understandings and elaborations of Wang's disciples about Mind and Principle, Mind-Body and Nature-noumenon, and noumenon and effort, and henceforth diversifications and their further developments.

1.　The Taizhou Sect[①]

Wang Yangming established his theory on the basis of innate knowledge. Innate knowledge was not only different from universal Principle, but also different from individual Mind, and its intrinsic characteristic was the unity of Mind and Principle. That "Mind is Principle" can be regarded as the generalization of this connotation. Logically speaking, the unity of Mind and Principle embodies the dual orientation of development: First, the restoration of universal Principle to individual Mind, or the interpretation of Principle with Mind; second, the restoration of individual Mind to universal Principle, or the interpretation of Mind with Principle. The first orientation of development reflects more concretely the theories of the Taizhou Sect and Li Zhi[②]. The Taizhou Sect put forth the theory of Idea as dominator of Mind, and regarded individual Idea as the first Principle. Li Zhi transformed innate knowledge into Child-Mind. The main difference of the theory of Child-Mind from innate knowledge is that it presented completely natural Mind (original Mind) of the self, and no longer regarded Principle as "the inside dominator (of Child-Mind)"; to some extent, Li Zhi regarded Mind as Principle. The relation between Mind and Principle is logically connected with the distinction between Mind and Nature. Principle as internal noumenon usually obtains the form of Nature-noumenon. The Taizhou Sect held that Idea dominated Mind, and Li Zhi transformed innate knowledge with Child-Mind; both meant unfolding and intensifying the dimension of

---

① Taizhou School, a philosophical school founded by Wang Gen on the basis of Wang Yangming's ideas. It led an emancipative trend in the late Ming Dynasty.
② Li Zhi (1527 – 1602), a philosopher, historian and writer of the late Ming Dynasty. He was known for his criticism of the Neo-Confucian views espoused by Zhu Xi.

individual embedded in Mind-Body. Different from the above orientations of development of the Wang Yangming school in the late Ming Dynasty, in the unity of Mind and Principle, Liu Zongzhou[1] paid more attention to the dimension of universal Principle, and his study is manifested as a kind of return to Nature-noumenon.

The Taizhou Sect is one of the most influential sects in Wang Yangming's school, and its ideological tendency is distinctively different from the orthodox Confucianism. Possibly because of this, Huang Zongxi in his *Academic Cases of the Confucian Scholars of the Ming Dynasty* excluded the Taizhou Sect from Wang Yangming's School, and listed it as a separate case. However, in spite of the fact that the Taizhou Sect cannot be included as a sect of the orthodox Confucianism, it should doubtlessly be listed as a sect in Wang Yangming's school in consideration of its lineage and ideological inheritance. The founder of the Taizhou Sect was Wang Gen[2], one of Wang Yangming's favourite disciples, and it was a legendary tale that Wang Yangming accepted Wang Gen as his student. At the time Wang Yangming was in Nanchang, and Wang Yin of Taizhou requested a meeting with Wang Yangming. He dressed himself in an ancient robe and an ancient hat, with a wooden tablet in hand and two poems as the visiting gift. Wang Yangming was somewhat surprised at Wang Yin's appearance, and asked him: "What kind of hat are you wearing?" Wang Yin replied: "A hat in the style of the ancient sage Youyu." Wang Yangming again asked: "What kind of robe are you wearing?" Wang Yin responded: "An imitation of Laolaizi's robe." After that, the two had a scholarly discussion for a long time. Wang Yin sighed in admiration, and knelt down to call himself a disciple. After his return, he thought it once more, and it seemed he was less sure of his conviction, so he returned the second day to see Wang Yangming again for repeated debates, before he was fully convinced. Wang Yangming told his other disciples: "I didn't have any excitement when I succeeded

---

[1] Liu Zongzhou (1578 – 1645), a Confucian scholar of the Ming Dynasty known for his criticism of the teachings of Wang Yangming.
[2] Wang Gen (1483 – 1541), a philosopher of the Ming Dynasty who popularized the teachings of Wang Yangming.

in leading my army to quell Prince Ning's rebellion. But this time, I do feel excited to talk with this man." (*Academic Cases of the Confucian Scholars in the Ming Dynasty,* vol.32) Wang Yin changed his name later to Wang Gen. When Wang Yangming returned to his hometown in Zhejiang, Wang Gen also followed him closely. Wang Gen later created the Taizhou Sect, which turned out to be one of the most important sects in Wang Yangming's school. Wang Gen had his own disciples and followers such as his younger clan brother Wang Dong[1] and his son Wang Bi. Luo Rufang, Zhou Rudeng, etc. were among the important followers in the ensuing generations of the sect.

Wang Gen was a man of unique individuality, as shown in his first visit to Wang Yangming, which was quite symbolical. His came in the ancient robe and hat, and his return for the debates for the second time though appearing somewhat affected, demonstrated his distinctive personality. Due to his personal traits, Wang Gen found himself much attuned to the principle of individuality of Mindology after he became Wang Yangming's student, and the disciples of the Taizhou Sect also basically followed this line of thinking.

Wang Yangming once put forward his theory of self-perfection, and attached considerable importance to self-realization. With this theory as the prerequisite, Wang Gen further proposed his theory of body-protection. "The understanding of body-protection must lead to the love of physical body as a treasure." (*Posthumous Collection of Mr. Wang Xinzhai*, vol.1) Body-protection in a broad sense manifests the identification and affirmation of the self. It is worth noting that Wang Gen since then connected the identification and affirmation of the self with physical body. In essence, "physical body" is opposed to universal essence, and symbolizes the individual existence of man. The exposition of the identity with the self from the aspect of body-protection means an emphasis on the existence of the individual. Therefore, Wang Gen's exposition of the self from the perspective of physical body differs obviously from the definition

---

[1] Wang Dong (1509 – 1581), one of the leading figures of the Taizhou School and a student of Wang Gen.

of "self" with universal essence. This kind of focus on the existence of the individual at the same time is connected with the function of self-affirmation.

Body-protection in a narrow sense can be interpreted as the protection of self-existence. In Wang Gen's view, whether or not self-existence was protected was determined by whether or not "others loved me", and whether or not "others loved me" depended on whether or not "I treated others with the Way of benevolence". Therefore, whether or not the existence of an individual is protected, after all, is decided by himself. It is right based on this point that Wang Gen proposed seeking self reliance without blaming heaven or others: "Therefore a superior man should seek self support and not blame heaven above or resent man on earth." (*Ibid.*) Here heaven and man refer to the extensive objects beyond oneself. Seeking self support without complaining about heaven or resenting man means that the fate of an individual is not dominated by external force but completely controlled by oneself. Generally speaking, independence or selection by oneself is usually connected with the quality of will. Wang Gen affirmed the function of individual in the relation between self and objects (others and external objects in a broad sense), bestowed independence on individuals, and also comparatively stressed the determination of will in the self.

Seeking self support mainly refers to the protection of the existence of the individual. Therefore, Wang Gen again regarded the self as the fundamentals of heaven, earth and all things of creation, and heaven, earth and all things of creation as incidentals. In this way, the self not only is the master of his own body, but also constitutes the basis of the existence of heaven, earth and all things of creation. Since "I" am the fundamental under heaven, then all things of creation depend on "me": "Once a man knows self-cultivation is the fundamental of the world and the country, then he understands that heaven, earth and all things of creation depend on himself, and not that he depends on heaven, earth and all things of creation." (*Ibid.*) Wang Yangming once put forth the theory: "Heaven and earth without innate knowledge of man cannot be regarded as heaven and earth." Wang Gen's theory of the dependence of all things of creation on the self is similar to Wang Yangming's theory to some extent. Nevertheless, Wang Yangming mainly focused on the construction of the world of meaning; at the same time, this relation of meaning again unfolded the oneness between heaven and man without a counterpart. With regard to the unity between heaven and man, "I" am also dependent on heaven, earth and all things of creation. In comparison, Wang Gen affirmed that heaven, earth and all things of creation depended on the self, and again stressed that "Self does not depend on heaven, earth and all things of creation." Therefore, he proposed that "no counterpart for the relation between heaven and man" must be understood as that the self unilaterally determined the non-self (heaven, earth and all things of creation).

This relation between the self and all things of creation also manifests itself in the social domain. In the well-known Huainan theory of the investigation of the world, Wang Gen further elaborated on it. In his view, the physical self was like "a quadrate ruler", while the world or the country was like "a quadrate". If we measure a quadrate with a quadrate ruler, we know then if a quadrate ruler is not straight itself, it cannot show a straight quadrate. Only after the quadrate ruler has been corrected and straightened first can a straight quadrate be drawn. Likewise, the self must first be properly cultivated in order to put the world and the country in good order. (*Ibid.*) The rectification of the world and the country with the physical self means regarding the self as the ultimate force that can determine the rise and fall, and chaos and order of the world and the country. It is worth noting here that Wang Gen still interpreted the self with the physical self, thus this self was different from the abstract Principlist subject. As a self-reliant determiner, the physical self in a certain sense manifests a will in action or an incarnation of will.

In correspondence to his attempt to promote the function of the self, Wang Gen formulated a new definition on the relation between the self and Fate: "Although my Fate is bestowed by heaven, it is I who shape and direct its development." (*Ibid*, vol. 2) Fate in Chinese philosophy is a rather complex concept. If its religious sense is ignored, Fate has the meaning of inevitability. Nonetheless, in the form of Fate, inevitability has some mysterious implication. In a narrow sense, "my Fate is predestined by heaven" originated from Kong Zi's belief that "There is Fate for life and death". It means life and death of any individual are predestined. In a broad sense, that Fate is predestined by heaven means that inevitable Fate exists independent of the self. In this latter sense, that "Fate is predestined by heaven" and "I shape and direct its development" means that although inevitable Fate is outside of myself, in the end it can be controlled and directed by myself. Wang Gen's disciple Luo Rufang further elaborated on the relation between the physical self and morality: "As soon the self is established, the Way of the universe reveals itself; as soon as the physical self moves, the Way of the universe starts to function." (*Important Quotations of Mr. Luo Jinxi*) In contrast to Fate, the Way has the meaning of universal law. That the establishment of the physical self can enable the Way to function means the universal laws are subjected to the self. From the point that the self shapes and directs Fate to the point that the establishment of the self can enable the Way to function, the function of self-determination is unfolded in all aspects in the relation between the self and the non-self.

As Wang Gen mainly based his theory on the promotion of the existence of the individual, and further emphasized that it was "I" who shaped and directed the development of Fate in consideration of the relation with external inevitability, another representative of the Taizhou Sect, Wang Dong focused more on the irrational dimension of the existence of the individual in the relation between Mind and Idea. He first endowed Idea with oriented function. (*Posthumous Collection of Mr. Wang Yi'an*, vol.1, briefly *Yi'an Collection* hereafter) Orientation indicates a concentrated one-dimensional tendency, and this kind of Idea with orientated function is different from a general idea: "And the Idea I mean is like the dominant Idea, and not an idea in general sense." (*Ibid.*) "Dominant" Idea in contrast to a general idea contains the meaning of self-determination. Qualifying "Idea" with "dominant" aims at emphasizing its character of self-determination. To sum up, the Idea in Wang Dong's theory indicates the unity of one-dimensional concentrated tendency (orientation) and self-determination, and its connotation is roughly equal to Wang Yangming's "will". In fact, Wang Dong himself already made a connection between the two: "When a will is oriented, it also means the dominator is fixed, then can a will be far away from an idea?" (*Ibid.*) It is not difficult to see that this Idea connected with the oriented will is already close to the category of will.

Idea as the unity of one-dimensional concentration (orientation) and self-determination is also called "independence", and it has the function of "self-decision, self-design and self-transformation". (*Ibid.*) Self-decision, self-design and self-transformation are also self-selection and self-determination of Idea, and it can be regarded as the concretization of the self-reliant quality of Idea. Obviously it is to some extent worth considering that Wang Dong here linked self-decision with "independence". "Independence" has not only the meanings of dependence on nothing and self-decision (independent decision), but also the meaning of isolation from other conscious phenomena. Logically speaking, defining Idea as "independence" means denying the restraint of factors (for instance, rationality) outside of will on will. Wang Dong confessed frankly about this, and thought that factors such as "experience and knowledge" and "feelings, interests and harms" should be extracted from Idea. (*Ibid.*)

Experience and knowledge refer to sensitive perception and rational thinking in general, while feelings, interests and harms are associated with the evaluation of value. With regard to the way of function, the choice and decision of will usually do not directly reflect the results of rational deduction or consideration of fame and gain, and there are indeed some factors of irrationality in them. It is based on this perception that Wang Dong held that Idea did not rely on experience and knowledge. However, that activity of will is not a direct product of experience and knowledge as well as judgments in consideration of fame and interests does not mean there is no connection between the two. In view of the real course, choice and decision of will are always in different ways connected with the understanding of Principle of necessity (truth), and the evaluation of relation of value (goodness). Wang Dong stressed that the activity of will could not be mixed with any knowing of experience and knowledge, and consideration of feelings, interests and harms. This unavoidably rejected the readjustment of will with the understanding of facts and the evaluation of value in favor of the self-determination of will. Once will extricates itself from the restraint of rationality, it usually evolves into a spiritual power of independence and absolute freedom. Here it shows certain tendency of voluntarism.

Independence is the internal definition of Idea. With regard to the relation between Idea and Mind, Wang Dong paid more attention to the connotation of the dominator of Idea: "For the dominator of the physical body of self is Mind, and the dominator of self Mind is Will." (*Ibid.*) This view involves a dual relation, i.e. Body versus Mind, and Mind versus Idea. Mind in opposition to physical Body generally refers to the subject's consciousness or spirit; Idea in opposition to Mind refers to Will as the unity of one-dimensional concentration and self-reliance. In terms of the relation between Body and Mind, Body is dominated by Mind; in terms of the relation between Mind and Idea, Will dominates the subject's consciousness (including rationality). Wang Dong compared Idea to the Extreme Ultimate, which means he bestowed on Idea a transcendental quality. In the form of the Extreme Ultimate, the "dominant" in the dominant Idea obtained new connotation: It began to proceed from self-decision to dominance of the subjective spirit.

The Taizhou Sect regarded the self as the first Principle from Wang Gen's theory of self-shaping and self-guidance in the development of Fate to Wang Dong's theory of dominance of Idea over Mind, and removed the restraint of universal Principlism on the activity of Will with the dominance of Idea of the individual. The development of this theory started from Wang Yangming's Mindology, and at the same time extended and intensified unidimensionally the individual principle embodied in the philosophy, thus manifesting a tendency of voluntarism. Huang Zongxi made such a comment on the Taizhou Sect: "After Taizhou (i.e. Wang Gen), many of his followers seemed to be able to combat dragons and monster-snakes bare-handed, and by the time of Yan Shannong and He Xinyin, they could no longer be confined within the scope of the doctrine of name and reality. ... Those scholars could shake heaven and earth. No predecessors and successors could be on a par with them. Chan Buddhists often beat with a stick or shouted loudly at will to show their wits promptly. Once they put down the stick, they were like idiots. But the scholars of the Taizhou Sect conducted themselves as if they carried loads in nude and never put them down; therefore, they did greater harms." (*Academic Cases of the Confucian Scholars in the Ming Dynasty*, vol.32) Here the doctrine of name and reality refers to universal Principlist norms in general, and being no longer confined within the doctrine of name and reality means breaking away from the restraint of Principlist norms. Abandoning the command of Principle of necessity and criteria of oughtness to emphasize the function of Idea of individual makes it difficult to avoid blind impulsion of will. Shaking heaven and earth, or carrying loads in nude, indeed demonstrated some irrational willpower.

The Taizhou Sect stressed Idea of individual, and it seems that in some aspect this theory was close to the Chan Buddhism that focused on self-mind; the closeness in form of the two sects often caused the Taizhou Sect to have been satirized as "unruly Chan Sect". Nevertheless, it is not difficult to see with some analysis that although there exist some similarities between the two, their theoretic tendencies in depth manifest different characteristics. The Chan Buddhism associated Mind with sudden enlightenment, and believed that once a man was enlightened to see his own Mind, he could attain the status that "anything he perceives is the Way with a free Mind". (*Commentary on the Sutra of Perfect Enlightenment*, vol.3, 2nd Bk.) The goal is to realize a living both in the present world and the super-mundane world at the same time through intuition from delusion to enlightenment. It not only manifests the tendency of intuitionism, but also implies a veiled recognition of the established order. On the contrary, the Taizhou Sect associated willpower with the subject's function on heaven, earth and all things of creation, and demanded "immediate efforts in appropriate divisions and adjustments of seasons to assist easy communion between heaven and earth, and contribution to the harmonious reproduction of all things of creation". (*Collection of Yi'an*, vol.1) In the view of the Taizhou Sect, the difference between the subject and grass, trees, fowls and beasts lay in its initiative consciousness with Idea as the dominator. It is this initiative power that determined the subject could control and make use of grass, trees, fowls and beasts. What this view stressed is not that "anything perceived is the Way", but "expansion of the Way". In a sense, it exalted the subject's initiative function in the form of voluntarism.

There is no doubt that some theoretic problems exist when the Taizhou Sect started from an emphasis of Idea of individual and led Mindology to voluntarism. Hegel once analyzed the function of will, called the abstract will without restriction of rationality "negative will", and maintained: "When it turns to be applied in reality, its state in politics and religion will be changed into a zeal of destroying all social orders." (*Principles of the Law Philosophy*, The Commercial Press, 1982, 14) Indeed it is easy for Idea of individual to evolve into a destructive force to intensify one-sidedly its function outside of Principle of necessity. Although the Taizhou Sect did not unite itself with any political force or religious power in reality and did not bring any real impact on the social order, in a logic point of view, it had the destructive tendency of shaking heaven and earth in stressing self-shaping and self-guidance in the development of Fate, Idea as dominator, and further, in its advocacy of "anything I do with the greatest freedom". (Luo Rufang)

In the perspective of history, however, the Taizhou Sect replaced the Chan Buddhism's theory that "anything perceived was the Way" with "expansion of the Way of non-action", and at the same time, it has another kind of meaning. Since the Han Dynasty, Confucianism gradually became the mainstream of Chinese culture. Although Confucianism did not deny the subject's function in self-realization, obedience to heavenly mandate and awe of heavenly mandate had always been the guiding concepts, and the latter gradually developed into the form of fatalism with the evolution of Confucianism. In the orthodox Principlism, this tendency of fatalism saw further development, and the orthodox Principlism transformed the criterion of oughtness metaphysically into the Principle of necessity, and nullified self-selection and self-decision with the dominance of the heavenly Principle, so that the subject's conduct possessed the fatalist attribute. In such a theoretic milieu, the Taizhou Sect affirmed that the subject was not passively obedient to heavenly mandate, but demonstrated the ability of dissemination, establishment and expansion of the Way, which is undoubtedly a challenge to the traditional fatalism. Wang Yangming once remarked: "It is only when the Will is familiar with regulations that a subject can follow his own inclinations without violation of them." (*Records of the Instructions and Reviews*, vol.1) Thus, he affirmed that the conduct should be the unity of submission to the Principlist norms and conformity to the internal Will. This emphasis on the Will of individual in terms of moral practice has transcended the horizons of the orthodox Principlism in regard to the heavenly Principle as established mandate. The Taizhou Sect to some extent followed the above line of thinking, and launched a further attack in an even more extreme means against the orthodox concepts of supreme heavenly mandate and absolute supremacy of heavenly Principle. In view of this aspect, the claim that the Taizhou Sect "can no longer be confined within the scope of the doctrine of name and reality" has its own unique historical significance.

2. The Theory of Child-Mind and the Principle of Individual

The intensification of the individual dimension in the Mindology of the Taizhou Sect is to a certain extent reflected in Li Zhi's theory. However, in comparison with the affirmation of individual existence (protection of body) of the Taizhou Sect, and further change mainly to the irrational dimension (Idea) of existence, Li Zhi's attention was always on the individual existence per se.

Li Zhi (1527-1602) was originally known as Lin Zaizhi. After his success in the provincial examinations, he changed his surname to Li, and again changed his name to Zhi for avoiding the taboo of the imperial name. His style names are Zhuowu, Hongfu, a Retired Wenling Scholar, a Retired Sizhai Scholar, etc. He is a native of Quanzhou. His ancestors once went overseas for trade, and his father was a private tutor. Li Zhi succeeded in the provincial examinations and received the title of "Juren" in 1522. He was once an erudite scholar at Nanjing Imperial College, assistant to Vice Minister of the Nanjing Ministry of Punishments and prefect of Yao'an Prefecture, Yunnan. He resigned his post at the age of 54 and lived in seclusion at Macheng, Hubei, devoting himself to writing and lecturing. In 1602, Emperor Shenzong of the Ming Dynasty issued a decree to arrest him for the crime of "boldly advocating rebellious ideas to confuse and instigate people". He committed suicide in prison with a razor.

Li Zhi used to follow Wang Bi, son of Wang Gen, as a student. He paid several visits to Luo Rufang, another student of Wang Gen, for discussion of academic issues. In terms of the master-student relation, his theory could not be separated from Wang Yangming's Mindology. Li Zhi especially held the Taizhou Sect in high esteem and commented: "At the time Master Yangming had disciples and students all over the country, only Master Xinzhai (Wang Gen) was the most brilliant." (To the Second Master of Huang'an, *On the Burning of Books*, vol. 2) Similar to the Taizhou Sect, Li Zhi especially elaborated on the individualistic principle in Mindology. Of course, the two had their own characteristics in the theoretic orientations.

Wang Yangming established his theory on the basis of Mind. Such emphasis on Mind-Body obviously influenced Li Zhi. It is not difficult to find it in Li Zhi's theory of Child-Mind: "The Child-Mind is a Mind of trueness." (Theory of Child-Mind, *On the Burning of Books*, vol.3) As the very first idea, Child-Mind has not only the meaning of the original state, but also the meaning of transcendence. With regard to the logical starting point in the system of transcendental Mind, there is no doubt that Li Zhi's view and Wang Yangming's theory were interconnected to some extent. However, as related previously, Wang Yangming's analysis of Mind and Nature aimed at solving the problem of how to attain the internal sagehood. The Mind-Body he re-established at the same time was regarded as the internal basis for the attainment of sagehood. In relation with it, in Wang Yangming's view, Mind-Body contains not only the definition of individuality, but also universal Principle as its content. In comparison with Wang Yangming, Li Zhi showed a different way of thinking. In Li Zhi's view, the top priority was not how an individual could attain sagehood, but how an individual could exist, and Child-Mind primarily was not the basis for the attainment of sagehood, but the basis of existence.

In Li Zhi's view, Child-Mind was firstly different from "experience and the Way and Principle". The experience and the Way and Principle in opposition to Child-Mind are not perceptive knowledge or rational knowledge in the epistemological sense, but take Principle as the basis (originating from Principle). Principle as the universal norm symbolizes chiefly the essence of Man. The orthodox ideology demands Principle serve as "internal dominance", and stresses the universal essence is an external determination of the individual. In Li Zhi's view, Child-Mind was the basis of the true existence of the individual, and the loss of Child-Mind meant loss of the true existence: "If Child-Mind is lost, then the true Mind is lost; since the true Mind is lost, then the true Man is lost." (*Ibid.*) The original Mind and true Mind emphasize the priority of the true existence of the individual over the transcendental essence. It is not difficult to see that behind replacing Principle with Child-Mind is the defense of the true existence of the individual.

Stress on the true existence of the individual means logically an affirmation of the value of the individual existence. Based on his theory of Child-Mind, Li Zhi put forward his proposition that every man could surely be useful in his own way: "Heaven gives birth to a man, and he will certainly be useful in his own way." (*On the Burning of Books,* vol.1) "Use" in a broad sense belongs to the axiological category. In the times of Li Zhi, Kong Zi was usually regarded as the model of ideal personality. Such a model of personality at the same time symbolized the incarnation of universal Principle. The orthodox ideology set Kong Zi as an ideal example (to be followed completely), and this meant cultivating self with the universal moral concept. In such a circumstance, the value of the individual was solely represented as the recognition of the abstract Principle. In opposition to this, Li Zhi advocated that a man would certainly have his usefulness, and affirmed every individual had his own internal value. It is from this point that Li Zhi further demanded self-establishment and self-contentedness. That shows his great concern for the dignity of the individual. If the self cannot be established, then it cannot face the world in which the individual exists. Jacob Burckhardt once pointed out that in the Middle Ages, "A man is only a member of a race, party, clan or community — He realized himself only through some general categories", while toward the time of the Renaissance, "Men became spiritual individuals, and also understood themselves in that way." (*Culture in the Italian Renaissance*, The Commercial Press, 1981, 125) Certainly the late Ming Dynasty that Li Zhi lived in did not reach the state of the Renaissance, but he stressed "a man", focused on independence, and obviously his theory was different from the orthodox concept that determined the individual with general categories like "Heavenly Principle", etc. From a focuse on existence to an emphasis of the dimension of the individual, Li Zhi exhibited a foresighted consciousness in a sense.

In connection with the advocacy of self-establishment, Li Zhi demanded non-patronization. He was quite resentful against the prevailing patronization (seeking patronage from others): "Contemporaries all seek patronage from others." (*On the Burning of Books*, vol.1) In the historical perspective, in correspondence with the natural economy was usually a dependence of men on men, and this kind of dependence usually was unfolded in the form of patriarchal and hierarchical relation. Patronization was shown as the restriction of the individual in the patriarchal and hierarchical relation. In terms of metaphysical sense, the relation between patriarchy and self manifested a relation between species and individual. Behind it was the opposition between the species-essence and the individual existence. Patronization in this sense also meant the dissolution of the individual existence by the species-essence. In Li Zhi's view, once the individual was reduced to dependence on others and lost his independence, he would inevitably suffer a degradation of self-value: "If a man is sheerly dependent on others, then he will not have his own views or power in his whole life." (*Ibid.*) From the affirmation of the usefulness of the individual (a man) to the demand of non-patronization, the individual dimension obtained more concrete historical substance, and its position was further fixed at the metaphysical level.

It is not difficult to see with some analysis the theoretic relation between Li Zhi's above views and Wang Yangming's Mindology. Wang Yangming's Mind-Body and innate knowledge, as related above, are different from Nature-nomenon and Heavenly Principle of the orthodox Principlism, simply because the theory embodied internally the definition of individuality. Based on this as a logical prerequisite, Wang Yangming put forth the theory of self-realization, and understood the cultivation of Moral Nature as a course of self-identification and self-affirmation. Related to self-realization is "to rise without expectation": Wang Yangming repeatedly recommended the quality of extraordinary men. The above orientations of Wang Yangming's Mindology not only affirmed the value of the self (subject) between the relation of subjects, but also paid attention to the aspect of the individual as a possible existence in the relation between existence and essence. There is no doubt that Li Zhi had inherited the above Mindological concept when he emphasized that a man would certainly have his own usefulness. However, in correspondence to the commitment to universal Principle in both Mind-Body and innate knowledge, in Wang Yangming's theory, self-realization usually led to the attainment of sagehood, while the ideal realm of existence was usually understood as a return to the essence. In contrast to this, it seems that Li Zhi presented a different way of thinking. In fact, when Li Zhi transformed Mind-noumenon (innate knowledge) with Child-Mind, he had latently set up his orientation of thinking that was different from Wang Yangming's: Child-Mind was mainly different from Wang Yangming's Mind-noumenon (innate knowledge) in that it had abandoned universal Principle. Starting from this point, Li Zhi paid more attention to the existence of the individual: the dimensions of individual existence from the internal spiritual noumenon to the external relation between self and others were all raised to most prominent positions.

Individual existence is not only a fact in the conceptual domain, but always unfolds in the relation between subjects in reality. In correspondence with the affirmation of the usefulness of every man, Li

Zhi advocated: "Emphasize selfism, and ensure self-convenience." Here selfism is mainly not self-realization of morality, but a general principle in dealing with the relation between men. In the form of emphasizing selfism and ensuring self-convenience, the self seems to have been elevated to the supreme position. This intensification of the self undoubtedly has some connection with the theory of the Taizhou Sect. However, the Taizhou Sect stressed the dimension of the self mainly in the relation between the Way of necessity and Idea of individual, while Li Zhi emphasized the supremacy of the self in the inter-subjective relation. Under the specific historical circumstance of the dark Middle Ages, Li Zhi's demand of "selfism" undoubtedly was meant to avoid the neglect of individual rights. Nevertheless, in terms of the relation between individual and community, over-emphasis on selfism also contained a tendency of neglecting the interests of community. It is not difficult to see this point in the following exposition by Li Zhi: "I study for myself and for my interests with a selfish Mind, and only for the convenience of myself directly and promptly." (*Collected Works of Li Wenling*, vol.4) As related above, Wang Yangming once tried to connect the self with the others in the form of oneness of all things of creation, and move from subject to inter-subjects. Although his standpoint of "non-self" made it difficult for the individual to genuinely obtain the appropriate position in the end, he demonstrated to a certain extent self-consciousness for the adjustment of the relation between subjects. In contrast with this, Li Zhi regarded "selfism" and "self-interest" as the only principle. It seems that he returned to the standpoint of subject from that of inter-subjects, or that subjectivity once again prevailed over inter-subjectivity. This in theory led to the internal tension in another form between the individual principle and the community principle.

The individual principle is embodied in the internal domain of Nature and Feeling, i.e. it is concretized as unaffectedness and non-violation against Nature. To put it elaborately, the self in the world should let go of feelings without hypocritical concealment (unaffectedness), let Nature develop in its natural state without external imposition (non-violation against Nature), not conceal Child-Mind of self (no evil-doing against Mind), and not violate the subject's internal will (no suppression of Will). In Li Zhi's view, if emotions are pent-up within self, a man can disclose them freely without restriction of manners. It is worth noting that Li Zhi connected internal will and disclosure of emotions with "self-esteem", which allowed unaffectedness and non-violation against Nature to assume the significance of self-identification and self-affirmation. The differences of individuals in the domain of Nature and Feeling determine that it is impossible to cultivate them in uniformity: "No one is without feelings, and no one is without personality. How can they be demanded to follow the same principles!" (Random Thoughts on Reading the Laws, *On the Burning of Books*, vol. 3) Just as selfism, self-interest, self-convenience emphasize the Principle of individuality mainly from the relation between self and others, that "Nature and Feeling cannot be demanded to follow the same principles" is unfolded as the same principle through the affirmation of the diversity of development in internal spiritual world.

In contrast to the demand of "temper Feeling with Nature" in the orthodox Principlism and self-discipline in the pure Confucian way, Li Zhi's above views doubtlessly inherited more from Wang Yangming's advocacy of "perfection with natural talent". Of course, in Li Zhi's theory, the irrational aspects of Feeling, Will, etc. were elevated to even higher positions. The free development of individuality began to replace the single pursuit of the realm of internal sagehood. Li Zhi's stress on the world of emotions and the diversity of personality exerted influence to some extent on the literature of the late Ming Dynasty. His contemporary, well-known dramatist Tang Xianzu, held Li Zhi in high esteem. Like Li Zhi, Tang Xianzu also regarded the dimension of emotions as a crucial aspect of the subject: "People always live for emotions. Emotions give birth to poetry, which exerts influence on the spirit of people. All talks, laughter, great things, trivial things, and life and death involve emotions." (An Essay on Er Bo's Visit to Magu, *ibid*. vol.31) This view corresponds to Li Zhi's unaffectedness and non-violation against personality, and constitutes the basic principle for Tang Xianzu's dramatic creation. Sometime later, Feng Menglong shared with Li Zhi's theory of Nature and Feeling, and applied it to the literary creation. The affirmation and praise of individual Feeling not only were the products of speculation and deduction, but also reflected the historical changes in the late Ming Dynasty, such as the initial rise of urban residents. If "Nature and Feeling cannot be demanded to follow the same principles" reflects at the philosophical level the longing for individual freedom at the strata of urban residents, then Tang Xianzu and Feng Menglong identified with the view and expressed the same will from the perspective of literary creation. In this sense, Li Zhi unfolded the principle of individuality in Mindology in the domain of Nature and Feeling, and obviously this again depended on the evolution of the society in the late Ming Dynasty as the background.

In general, with the theory of Child-Mind as the prerequisite of ontology, Li Zhi turned the focus of Mindology from the attainment of sagehood to the existence of the individual. Through the emphasis on the definition of individuality in Mind-Body and innate knowledge, and the removal of the universal Principle, the existence of the individual began to obtain priority over universal essence. Meanwhile, in the propositions such as "Heaven gives birth to a man, and he will certainly have his own usefulness", "Emphasize selfism and ensure self-convenience", and "Nature and Feeling cannot be demanded to follow the same principles", the individual dimension is further unfolded in different orientations of existence. This theoretical orientation begins with Wang Yangming's Mindology as the logical starting point, but it cannot be totally included in the scope of Mindology. It promotes and intensifies the principle of individuality, and at the same time displays the tendency of unconditional rejection of universal Principle and universal essence. While Wang Yangming in his reconstruction of Mind-Body had already bespoken a deviation from essentialism to some extent, Li Zhi's theory of Child-Mind expressed an even more direct rebellion against essentialism. The latter also determined the heterodoxy of his thought. There undoubtedly exists a historical rationality in Li Zhi's emphasis on existence and his call for individuality. However, in the theoretical perspective, his way of thought also has its own limitations in the positioning of existence and essence, and the principle of individuality and the principle of universality.

3.　Return to Nature-Noumenon

After the Taizhou Sect and Li Zhi, Liu Zongzhou made further study on Mind and Nature, and the relevant relations between existence and essence, individuality and universality, idea and knowledge, etc. Liu Zongzhou (1578-1645) was a native of Shanyin (present Shaoxing, Zhejiang), and had style names of Qidong and Niantai. Since he used to lecture at the Jishan Mountain, he was addressed as Master Jishan by scholars. He became a would-be official in the year of *xinchou* (1601) in the reign of Emperor Wanli. His highest official position was the chief procurator of Nanjing Government. After the fall of the Southern Ming Dynasty, he died of a 20-day hunger strike.

Liu Zongzhou once was a student of Xu Fuyuan (Xu Jing'an), who criticized the theories of the Taizhou Sect but highly recommended Wang Yangming's Mindology. This academic relation of teacher and student right from the start brought Liu Zongzhou in theoretic contact with Mindology. Of course, in the formation of his theory, Liu Zongzhou had changed his attitudes to Mindology several times, and once he even "argued and questioned about it". The argumentation and questioning can be regarded as elaboration, correction and reinterpretation of Mindology. The focus Liu Zongzhou paid attention to in his life was basically within the domain of Mind and Nature. With regard to the evolution of Mindology, the point worth noting in his thought is first in the study of Mind and Nature. While the Taizhou Sect and Li Zhi elaborated on the dimension of the individual within Mind-Body from different aspects, Liu Zongzhou emphasized the dimension of universality of Mind-Body, and exhibited certain tendency of returning to Nature-noumenon.

Liu Zongzhou in his study of Mind and Nature regarded the analysis of Mind as the logical prerequisite. Mind as a philosophical category has relatively complex connotations, and Liu Zongzhou's definition of Mind correspondingly involves multiple aspects. In Liu Zongzhou's view, Mind should base itself on Nature, and unite with Nature. If Mind was studied without Nature, then Mind was only a kind of intelligent apperception. However, intelligent apperception is a kind of rational ability and activity, and it does not involve any concrete substance. Nature as noumenon of Principlism is not an empty thing without substance. It has not only the meaning of form, but also the meaning of essence. In essence, Nature always reflects certain moral relation, and concretely presents itself as the internalization of the criterion of oughtness. In Liu Zongzhou's view, if the definition of Nature was abstracted from Mind, then it could only be intelligent apperception. Only in unity with Nature could Mind obtain concrete moral substance, and be further promoted as substantial ethical noumenon. It can be seen that Mind in combination with Nature has transcended its original state to become the concrete state of oughtness. The Mind-Body in this sense is in fact nothing but a different expression of Nature-noumenon, while the interpretation of Mind with Nature means further emphasis on Principlist noumenon.

Liu Zongzhou's philosophical construction took Wang Yangming's Mindology as the logical starting point. As related previously, Wang Yangming established his theory on innate knowledge, and also defined innate knowledge with "Mind is Principle". That Mind was Principle embraced internally different dimensions of interpretation, and it was concretely embodied in the course of evolution of Wang's Mindology in the late Ming Dynasty. The Taizhou Sect explained the dimension of individual Mind in "Mind is Principle" in the perspective of the individual will, and Li Zhi in his theory of Child-Mind presented a similar tendency in the way of rejecting Principle. Over-intensification of Principlism usually led to despotism of Principlism and essentialism, and the orthodox Chengs-Zhu's Principlism in their emphasis on transcendental Principle unavoidably demonstrated the above tendencies. In the debates between Heavenly Principle and human desire, and Mind of Man and Mind of the Way, etc., it is not difficult to see this point. In regard to this prerequisite, the unfoldment of the dimension of individual Mind has the significance of restricting Principlist despotism and essentialism. In theory, it also helps to bring attention to the diversity of subjective consciousness and the value of individual existence.

In opposition to the Principlist despotism and essentialism, some of the followers of Wang Yangming's school, however, usually could not find appropriate positions for universal Principle and general Principlist norms. Wang Ji[①], Wang Yangming's own student, once put forward the theory of existing innate knowledge. The existing innate knowledge is based on the theory of four-nons (i.e. non-goodness and non-evil of Mind, Idea, Knowledge and Matter). Goodness in Principlism has the meaning of practical Principlism, and non-goodness means removing the Principlist substance, which may lead to regarding natural Feeling and Idea as innate knowledge. In the theory of the Taizhou Sect, the original innate knowledge is regarded as existing innate knowledge and united with the emphasis on Feeling and Idea, which gradually led to the impracticality of Principlist norms. Li Zhi even more firmly rejected Principle with original Child-Mind, and from here he deducted the theory of non-definiteness of right and wrong, and the relativist conclusion that "This right and that wrong do not harm each other", thus further dissolving Principlist noumenon. It has been mentioned above that Huang Zongxi once criticized that the Taizhou Sect "could not be confined within the scope of the doctrines of name and reality". Here the doctrines of name and reality include Principlist norms in a broad sense. Behind the unconfinability of the doctrines of name and reality is the proposal that individual Feeling and Idea are raised above Principlist noumenon. This tendency in theory seems to reach another extreme in opposition to Principlist despotism.

Liu Zongzhou noticed this evolution of Wang Yangming's philosophy in the late Ming Dynasty, and criticized: "Nowadays people everywhere talk about innate knowledge. Even its weaknesses the unruly scholars mixed with Feeling, and all knowledge is also called innate knowledge." (Random Notes on Verification and Understanding in Study, *Complete Collection of*

---

① Wang Ji (1498 – 1583), a philosopher of the Ming Dynasty. A student of Wang Yangming's, he founded the Zhejiang School to spread Wang's ideas.

Liuzi, vol.6) Feeling and Knowledge generally refer to individual Feeling and Idea, which are often connected with the irrational aspects of the individual consciousness. The theory of Feeling and Knowledge as innate knowledge is the logical extension of the theory of four-nons and the theory of existing innate knowledge, and along with this development are the loss of Principlist noumenon and the elation of non-Principlism. Liu Zongzhou interpreted Mind with Nature, and stressed Nature-noumenon, which can be regarded as a theoretic response to the above situations in the academic circle of the late Ming Dynasty, and his intention was to reconstruct Principlist noumenon and restore the esteem of Principlism. In the situation that individual Feeling and Knowledge prevailed over Principlist innate knowledge, the effort of Liu Zongzhou obviously had the significance of rectifying the deviations: Liu Zongzhou led the focus of the contemporary theory to the universal essence of "man as a man" with a considerable level of historical self-consciousness, and demonstrated his solemn defense of Principlism and humanity. Liu Zongzhou once wrote *A Genealogy of Man*, and established the standard of Man, and his theme also aimed at the promotion of Principlist noumenon and effort. As the last Principlist of the late Ming Dynasty, Liu Zongzhou established his historical position primarily because of his call for returning to Principlism.

However, there are also theoretic problems for Liu Zongzhou's way of thinking. Different from the Taizhou Sect and Li Zhi, Liu Zongzhou regarded Nature as Mind, and focused on the dimension of universal Principle in "Mind is Principle". Through an emphasis on Nature-noumenon, Liu Zongzhou certainly restricted the overstepping of non-Principlism, but his demand of transforming Mind into Nature also manifested the tendency of restoring Mind to Principle. In the situation of regarding Nature as Mind and transforming Mind into Nature, the aspect of non-Principlism in subjective consciousness seemed to be dissolved in Principlism, while the dominance of Principlism would easily turn to be Principlist despotism. Principlism symbolizes the universal essence of Man, while the non-Principlist aspects, such as Feeling, Idea and Desire, are often associated with the existence of the individual. When

Man becomes an abstract incarnation of Principlism, it will be difficult to obtain the reasonable position for the existence of Man. It seems that Liu Zongzhou's way of thinking in a sense returned to Chengs-Zhu's theory from Wang Yangming's philosophy. In fact, on the distinction between Nature and Mind, Liu Zongzhou in his late years indeed criticized Wang Yangming, and thought he "did not analyse Nature." (The Original Meaning, On Study, *Complete Collection of Liuzi*, vol.7) It is not difficult to see in connection with the previous text that this kind of criticism is to a great extent an expression on the standpoint of Chengs-Zhu. While the Taizhou Sect ignored Nature-noumenon by emphasizing Feeling, Idea, etc., Liu Zongzhou regarded Nature as Mind, transformed Mind into Nature to emphasize Nature-noumenon, and more or less emptied the concept of Mind-Body. Therefore, it is still a difficulty in theory to handle in an acceptable way the relations between Principlism and non-Principlism, and existence and essence.

4. Unfoldment of the Theory of Attaining Innate Knowledge

In Wang Yangming's Mindology, in correspondence to the dual connotation of Mind-Body was the distinction between transcendental innate knowledge (noumenon) and the course of attainment of innate knowledge (effort), and the latter embodied different dimensions of the evolution of the theory of attaining innate knowledge. Among the followers of Wang Yangming's school, Wang Ji and the Taizhou Sect made analysis on a priori noumenon in multiple aspects. However, because of this, they equated noumenon with existing innate knowledge. Nie Bao, Luo Hongxian, etc., opposed to regarding noumenon as existing innate knowledge, but at the same time tried to return to the silent and unconscious noumenon. The two in different aspects displayed the dimension of apriority of innate knowledge. On the contrary, Qian Dehong, Ouyang De, etc., and the scholars of the Donglin Sect[1] at the

---

[1] Donglin School, an ideological and philosophical movement of the late Ming Dynasty headed by Gu Xiancheng and Gao Panlong. It advocated Confucian traditions and venerated the Cheng brothers and Zhu Xi.

end of the Ming Dynasty focused their attention on a posteriori effort, and made a study of the course of attaining innate knowledge from different aspects.

Wang Ji should be the first to be mentioned. Wang Ji (1498-1583) had the style names of Ruzhong and Longxi. In the second year (1523) of the reign of Emperor Jiajing, he became a student of Wang Yangming, and was one of the most intelligent among the students. At that time, many people came from different places to seek instructions, and Wang Ji and Qian Dehong often gave first lectures on the purports of Wang Yangming's Mindology. Therefore they were called instruction masters. Wang Ji later lectured in Jiangsu, Zhejiang, and other places; even at about 90, he was still writing academic works.

Wang Ji, as a follower of Wang Yangming, also established his theory on the basis of innate knowledge. In his view, innate knowledge was manifested concretely as a unity of apriority and apperception. It is this unity that determined that the self could "react at an inspiration" in real moral practice, i.e. prompt direct response on the basis of the innate understanding of innate knowledge. Here, apriority (bestowal of heaven) constitutes the source of the subject's apperception, while the subject's apperception in turn proves apriority of innate knowledge. In other words, apperception of the subject is completely dissolved in apriority of innate knowledge.

It is obvious that Wang Ji's views are different from those of Wang Yangming. One of the prerequisites in Wang Yangming's theory of attaining innate knowledge is the distinction between original knowledge (a priori innate knowledge) and apperceptive knowledge (self-consciousness of innate knowledge): Innate knowledge at first is not consciously realized by the subject, and only through the course of a posteriori attainment of innate knowledge could it be transformed into self-conscious knowledge. Wang Ji's theory is different in that the unity of apriority and apperception began to replace the distinction between naturalness and self-consciousness. Innate knowledge as the unity of naturalness and apperception was then the "existing innate knowledge".

Wang Yangming's affirmation of the unity of Mind and Principle, and noumenon and effort already demonstrated the tendency of sublating transcendence of noumenon, while Wang Ji's emphasis on oneness of apriority and apperception allowed innate knowledge to change further from the domain of transcendence to the realm of reality. In consideration of this, Wang Ji interpreted innate knowledge as something existing, and did not completely depart from Wang Yangming's line of thinking. Once innate knowledge became existing, its way of function would also correspondingly approach reality. In the relation between the subject and the external environment, the subject did not passively accept the function of the environment, but was in the dominant position, while the prerequisite of this dominance was the present apperception of innate knowledge. It is on the internal basis of this clear intelligence that the subject could observe and self-examine consciously the conduct in the external environments, and thus make judgment and choice to avoid passive changes in accordance with "situations". Here, the existing state of innate knowledge constitutes the real prerequisite for the self as a subject in this world.

Innate knowledge as the internal subjective consciousness is noumenon itself. In correspondence to the affirmation of the existing state of innate knowledge, Wang Ji opposed the discussion about effort apart from noumenon in the relation between noumenon and effort: "To discuss effort apart from noumenon can be regarded as a different way, and because of the difference, it is discrete." (*Complete Collection of Mr. Wang Longxi*, vol.9) Study of effort apart from noumenon not only means the neglect of the internal basis for the cultivation of Moral Nature, but also leads to the deviation from the regulation of noumenon over the course of the cultivation of Moral Nature. Effort made from this point is usually trivial and complicated. Only with innate knowledge as the dominator could it have its own orientation. In general, the relation between noumenon (innate knowledge) and effort are reflected in two aspects: First, noumenon (innate knowledge) as "present" conscious structure guarantees the unity of the subject's consciousness (always maintains the orientation of goodness in different situations), and the latter at the same time makes it possible to maintain the consistence of the subject's conduct. In comparison with Wang Yangming's connection of the function of innate knowledge (noumenon) and the course, Wang Ji stressed the established relation between noumenon and effort.

The self in the world exists always in mutual interaction with the society (environment). In the perspective of the domain of morality, this kind of function takes as its medium the self-consciously moral conscious structure of the subject: All kinds of social (environmental) factors can restrict the subject's value judgments, moral feelings and concrete conducts only through the subject's conscious structure formed in certain period, while the subject's acceptance and rejection of and identity with external norms are always based on the moral consciousness attainable at the present stage. It is this real (established) conscious structure that guarantees in one aspect the maintenance of the subject's constancy in moral judgment and conduct. If the function of the conscious structure of the subject as a medium is neglected, then it usually leads to a dual result in theory: Either like the extreme behaviourism, it leads to environmental fatalism; or it is difficult to realize the internal unity of personality. In regard to this aspect, Wang Ji emphasized taking present clear intelligence as the dominator, and objected to changing in accordance with situations and discussing effort apart from noumenon. Obviously he was insightful. There is no harm in saying that in the form of present innate knowledge, Wang Ji tried further to sublate the transcendental tendency embedded in apriority, led innate knowledge to the conscious domain of experience, and thereby stressed the function of established structure of moral consciousness in the subject's course of life.

Nevertheless, while he emphasized immediacy, presence and establishment of innate knowledge, it seems that Wang Ji could not completely distinguish innate knowledge from daily consciousness, and because of this it is difficult for the aspect of universality and transcendence of moral noumenon to obtain an appropriate definition. When innate knowledge is given an existing form, and equated to its present function, noumenon is correspondingly, more or less, dissolved into daily consciousness. This theoretic thinking in a sense is already close to the Chan Buddhism's "function as Nature", and Wang Ji indeed often received the criticisms of "being close to the Chan Buddhism". Meanwhile, the existing state of noumenon also makes a posteriori effort impractical. Luo Hongxian (Nian'an), also a follower of Wang Yangming, pointed out incisively: "To talk about noumenon all day long without mentioning effort. Once someone touches the topic of effort, he will immediately be condemned as heretic. Even if Master Yangming was alive today, he would have knitted his brows at them." (Letter to Wang Longxi, *Collected Writings of Mr. Luo Nian'an*, vol.3). It is obvious that this criticism was not groundless.

The above orientation of development of the theory of existing innate knowledge was manifested more concretely in the theory of the Taizhou Sect. In correspondence with the emphasis on Idea of the individual, the Taizhou Sect also stressed the presentness of innate knowledge. Wang Dong held: "There is no time for innate knowledge to be in unconsciousness, so there is no need to attain it with more efforts; i.e. there is no time for bright Moral Nature to be concealed, so there is no need to brighten it." (*Posthumous Collection of Mr. Wang Yi'an*, vol.1) That there is no time for innate knowledge to be in unconsciousness refers to that innate knowledge always exists in the subject in an existing state, and that there is no need to attain it with more efforts means the separation of noumenon from effort. It is the Taizhou Sect that first associated the presentness of innate knowledge with daily practice: "Innate knowledge is an inborn nature that every person has a fair share of from the antiquity to the present; he draws from it and uses it in daily life." (Reply to Zhu Sizhai Mingfu, *Collection of Xinzhai*, vol.2) Infiltration of existing innate knowledge into daily practice means that innate knowledge is not a transcendental noumenon, but is embodied and unfolded in daily moral practice. Moral consciousness always exhibits itself in the external world through the subject's conduct, which confers an attribute of worldliness in the subject's pursuit of moral ideal, and gives internal Moral Nature a quality in reality. It is in seeing this point that the Taizhou Sect demanded the application (use) of innate knowledge to daily ethical life. Of course, the connection between innate knowledge and daily practice also embodies the return of noumenon to the consciousness of daily practice. In this aspect, the Taizhou Sect and Wang Ji doubtlessly have some similarity in their ways of thinking.

Different from Wang Ji and the Taizhou Sect that developed their theories from the transcendental noumenon to existing innate knowledge, other followers of Wang Yangming's school focused their attention on the effort in attaining innate knowledge. Nie Bao (Shuangjiang) and Luo Hongxian (Nian'an) objected to regarding innate knowledge as established (present) innate knowledge, and at the same time stressed the difference between innate knowledge and established consciousness to metaphysicize noumenon; by insisting on returning to quietude as the effort to attain innate knowledge, they more or less led Mindology to the transcendental approach. Those who elaborated Wang Yangming's course of attainment of innate knowledge in a broader scope were Ouyang De (Nanye), Qian Dehong (Xushan), Zou Shouyi (Dongkuo), Chen Jiuchuan (Mingshui), etc., as representatives of the Effort Sect and the Donglin Scholars in the late Ming Dynasty.

According to the view of the Effort Sect, although innate knowledge was the a priori noumenon, its presentation could not be separated from a posteriori activity. As to this, Ouyang De expounded: "It is because of innate knowledge that man becomes the heart of heaven and earth, and the spirit of all things of creation. Therefore, in different social stratums and daily practice, great men observe celestial phenomena and terrestrial patterns, and have communion with spirits and deities for the development of all things of creation; common people make use of heaven and earth in various environments, stipulate regulations and follow them with prudence in order to support their parents. They all use nothing but innate knowledge. Without heaven, earth and men, there will not be daily experience such as sight and sound, thought and worry, communion and exchange, neither will there be innate knowledge." (*Collected Writings of Mr. Ouyang Nanye*, vol.1) The daily practice here generally refers to the course of mutual interaction (communion) between the subject and the external objects, and activities of perception, thinking, etc. in this course. In the course of the subjects' practical activities (with different stratums in daily practice), the internal innate knowledge gradually reveals itself. Without the course of daily practice, there will be no way for innate knowledge to present itself. That "there is no innate knowledge without daily practice" points out the meaning.

In regard to the affirmation of the connection between innate knowledge and daily practice/experiential activity, the above views of the Effort Sect and the theory of existing innate knowledge doubtlessly have similarities. In fact, in the aspect of rejecting the transcendence of innate knowledge, the Effort Sect and the theory of existing innate knowledge indeed share some common expressions. However, while the theory of existing innate knowledge stressed the presentness of innate knowledge to dissolve moral noumenon in spontaneous experiential consciousness, the Effort Sect never gave up its commitment to the dimension of universality and the dimension of self-consciousness of innate knowledge. As for the Effort Sect, innate knowledge revealed itself in daily practice, which mainly indicated that innate knowledge was not quiet and unconscious transcendental noumenon, but this did not mean that innate knowledge could be equated with daily incidental ideas. It is based on this standpoint that the Effort Sect criticized the theory of existing innate knowledge: "It stimulated the beginners who caught a first glimpse of its influence to speak outright and establish their own faultless realm. They were just contented with their prejudiced essence, and felt convenient in their habitual daily practice; therefore, they thought that they conducted themselves according to their own Nature and Mind. On the contrary, the effort was despised as triviality that made innate knowledge something increasingly subtle and indispensable, which knew right and wrong, and which was relied on to be apperceptive to realize true attainment, while the pursuit of wrong and the respect of fault were affirmed without return. The malpractice had certainly not merely been just like the old discrete habitual ways!" (Chen Jiuchuan: Letter to Wang Longxi, *Academic Cases of the Confucian Scholars in the Ming Dynasty*, vol.19) Contentment with their prejudiced essence and convenience in their habitual daily practice mean that they held the established spontaneous consciousness as noumenon, restricted themselves narrowly in their daily practice, and refused Principlist sublimation. In contrast, the Effort Sect stressed the self-conscious course of "knowing right and wrong, and being apperceptive to realize true attainment."

It is hard to say that the above views of the Effort Sect have provided any new views in theory, but in the perspective of the evolution of Mindology, it certainly has the significance that cannot be neglected. As related before, when the Taizhou Sect sublated the transcendence of noumenon, it also accepted the tendency of regarding spontaneous daily consciousness as innate knowledge, and thereby dissolved the Principlist efforts of study, inquiry, thinking and analysis. Nie Bao and Luo Hongxian held innate knowledge as quiet noumenon, and regarded the return to quietude as the way of attaining innate knowledge. Therefore, in a sense, they were oriented towards the mysterious experiential enlightenment. Although the two evolved in different orientations, they shared some similarity in the deviation from the dimension of Principlism. In such a milieu, the Effort Sect stressed the discreet effort of thinking and analysis and without doubt it showed their defense of Principlism.

The affirmation of effort in attaining innate knowledge is the prerequisite of the attainment of noumenon, and it mainly exhibits the relation between effort and noumenon in one aspect. In a different aspect, the effort of attaining innate knowledge itself must be based on noumenon: "Without the understanding of innate knowledge as noumenon, there is nothing solid as a basis for the effort of attaining innate knowledge." (Reply to Chen Mingshui, *Collection of Nanye*, vol.1) Noumenon as the basis means regulating the effort of attaining innate knowledge with innate knowledge. In regard to the aspect of noumenon and effort, noumenon undoubtedly constitutes the starting point, and its tendency of thinking is to interpret effort with noumenon. It seems that the latter is similar in form to the theory of existing innate knowledge. However, behind the similarity in form exist profound differences in the theoretic purports.

In the theory of existing innate knowledge, noumenon as the established and present form constitutes the starting point of daily practice. In contrast to it, the Effort Sect affirms the restriction of noumenon on the effort with the theory of the course as its theoretic prerequisite. In the dynamic perspective, the relation between noumenon and effort is always unfolded as a course of constant mutual interaction, and its concrete content is: to attain apperception of innate knowledge through the effort in the attainment of innate knowledge, and again to restrict and guide the effort with apperception of noumenon. Zou Shouyi once wrote a brief generalization: "Inability to make effort means inability to attain noumenon, and inability to attain noumenon is not effort." (Second Reply to Nie Shuangjiang, *Collected Writings of Mr. Zou Dongkuo*, vol.6) From the positive side, inability to make effort is inability to attain noumenon, i.e. to attain noumenon through effort; inability to attain noumenon is not effort, i.e. to follow noumenon further to attain knowledge. According the Effort Sect's view, this dynamic course of unity between noumenon and effort possesses the attribute of infinity. This kind of understanding of the relation between noumenon and effort can be regarded as the further unfoldment of Wang Yangming's theory of the course of the attainment of innate knowledge.

The noumenon in Mindology is in a sense a transcendentalized subjective conscious system and cognitive structure (including moral cognition), while the effort of the attainment of innate knowledge involves the course of cultivation of Moral Nature and cognition of moral knowledge. In the form of reality, it is in essence an interactive course between the subject's established conscious structure and cultivation of Moral Nature and moral cognition: Cultivation of Moral Nature and moral cognition always take the established conscious structure and cognitive conditions as their internal basis, for they do not start from nothing. In another aspect, the conscious structure itself is not unchangeable, as it always obtains new content and constantly improves itself along with the development of a posteriori effort. The Effort Sect interpreted innate knowledge as a course of exerting efforts to realize noumenon, and following noumenon to further attain innate knowledge. It has doubtlessly gained, more or less, some insight of interaction between internal conscious structure, and moral cognition and cultivation of Moral Nature. Of course, when the Effort Sect affirmed the dynamic unity of noumenon and effort, it had never given up the presupposition of apriority of noumenon. Therefore, it could not have in theory transcended the speculation of Mindology.

5. The Donglin Sect and Mindology

The Donglin Sect rose in the late Ming Dynasty. Its chief representatives were Gu Xiancheng, Gao Panlong, etc., who once lectured at the Donglin Academy and were hence called "the Donglin Sect". The Donglin scholars paid attention to the current political situations, and stressed the application of theories to the governance of the country. Their theory was historically related to Mindology: Gu Xiancheng's teacher is the second-generation disciple of Wang Yangming, and this academic teacher-student relationship indicates the Donglin Sect (with Gu Xiancheng as a leader) was more or less under the influence of Wang Yangming's Mindology.

When the Donglin Sect rose, the influence of Wang Ji's theory of existing innate knowledge had not faded out. The characteristic of the theory of existing innate knowledge was to stress noumenon and reject effort, and it inevitably resulted in insubstantiality. In regard to this deviation, Gu Xiancheng criticized that in the theory of existing innate knowledge, noumenon was something imaginary and separated from effort. It would certainly lead to a denial of the moral practice of doing good and rejecting evil with the theory of present innate knowledge as the starting point.

While criticizing the theory of existing innate knowledge, the Donglin scholars elaborated Wang Yangming's emphasis on the theory of effort. Gu Xiancheng compared Wang Yangming's theory of attainment of innate knowledge with Meng Zi's theory of innate knowledge, and maintained that after Wang Yangming added the word "attain" before innate knowledge, the connotation of the phrase became "the most precise", because it could prevent people from adopting the orientation of metaphysical emptiness. Gao Panlong also opposed the "overall emphasis on quietude", and stressed that "Learning can be conducive only when it is put into self-practice." Even when one read books, he should on one hand think over and understand them, and on the other hand devote himself to practice. What is worth noting is that the Donglin Sect combined self practice with country governance in reality. One of the entries in the *Donglin Declaration* is that the scholars "shall engage themselves in the discussion of political events in reality", i.e. the discussion of governance of the state affairs.

Study for state governance as the goal demands a concern for social order and people's suffering. In the view of the Donglin scholars, a man should not just pursue official promotion and noble titles, and should not stress only self-cultivation of Mind and Nature, but should care about the people and the social welfare. This in fact extends the effort of attainment of innate knowledge from daily moral practice to the governance of the country and the pacification of people. Gao Panlong talked even more concretely about this point, and held that even without any official position in the government ("living in the distant countryside"), a man should all the time think of the people in the country ("everything done must be for our people"). Here, the course of learning is unfolded not only through the activity of state governance for the people to attain self-consciousness of innate knowledge, but also through the application of practical knowledge to state governance to realize political ideal.

The above views of the Donglin scholars obviously deserve our attention. Practical governance of the country is different from moral practice of individual, for it is a kind of social activity with involvement of multiple relations. As a kind of social activity, it is essentially in a historical course. When the Donglin scholars connected learning and effort with practical governance of the country, it meant a consideration of the relation between effort and noumenon in the broad perspective of social activity. Before them, what Wang Yangming and the later scholars of the Effort Sect understood of effort was limited mainly within moral practice, such as serving parents and respecting elder brothers, while the Donglin scholars understood learning and effort in a broad sense as real affairs of state governance. Hence, they extended the domain of the effort of attainment of innate knowledge.

The Donglin scholars focused their attention on the governance of state affairs, which is of course not only the logical result of theoretical evolution but had profound social and historical origins. When the Chinese feudal society stepped into the late Ming Dynasty, it had already fallen into decline. There were the corruption in the government, the aggravation of land annexation, and the increasing threats of invasion caused the constant intensification of social contradictions. Therefore, the whole society was threatened by growing crises. These social phenomena worried the Donglin scholars greatly and stimulated their commitment to social reformation. The criticisms on the empty talks on noumenon and the stress on the practical affairs of state governance can be regarded as the concretization of this consciousness of commitment.

Chapter Four

Mindology at the Turn of the Ming and Qing Dynasties

At the turn of the Ming and Qing Dynasties, significant historic changes took place. In addition to a dynastic change, there was also a more profound transformation in different aspects of economy, culture, etc. With the drastic social turbulence as background, the thinkers on the whole began a historical retrospection, and made thorough researches on Mindology, including Wang Yangming's, since the Song and Ming Dynasties. Some thinkers, such as Gu Yanwu and Wang Fuzhi, made multi-faceted criticisms of Mindology (especially its last period of development) from outside of it. Some other thinkers started their studies from Mindology and went out of its scope, and among them Huang Zongxi is the most representative one.

Huang Zongxi (1610-1695), styled as Taichong, Nanlei and Lizhou, was from Yuyao of Zhejiang. He followed Liu Zongzhou as a student in his early years. At the time when the Qing troops invaded the Ming territory and marched to the south, he led an army to resist them. After the fall of the Ming Dynasty, he resigned from all official posts and devoted himself to writing as a recluse. In his late years he restored Liu Zongzhou's Zhengren Academy, and gave lectures to students there. He was erudite in astronomy, calendar calculation, music, classics and history books, and works of philosophers. He had a profound knowledge in historiography, and was the pioneer of the historiography of east Zhejiang in the Qing Dynasty. Zhang Xuecheng pointed out that Huang Zongxi "had academically inherited the thought of Wang Yangming and Liu Zongzhou, and was followed by Wan Sitong and Wan Sida". This observation is not entirely groundless. At the same time, when Huang Zongxi studied under Liu Zongzhou, he also accepted the influence of Wang Yangming's Mindology, and in many aspects, his thoughts were related to it. Of course, when Huang Zongxi learned Mindology, he repeatedly went beyond its scope, and his thought was no longer restricted in Mindology.

In the relation between Mind and Nature, Huang Zongxi put forth the theory that Nature was seen only in Mind: "Nature cannot be seen; it can only be seen in Mind." (*On Master Meng Zi*, vol.2) That Nature can only be seen in Mind means that the universal noumenon is always embodied in the Mind of the individual. With this as the prerequisite, Huang Zongxi maintained a different view from the theory of Nature and Feeling in the orthodox Principlism. Feeling belongs to the category of Mind in a broad sense, and the relation between Nature and Feeling can be regarded as the concretization of the relation between Mind and Nature. The orthodox Principlism regards Nature as noumenon, and interprets Nature apart from Feeling (Mind), thus leading to the transcendentalization of noumenon. The so-called "suspended object" is such a transcendental noumenon. Huang Zongxi held that Nature and Feeling could not be divided for study, and what he emphasized was the unity of universal Nature and individual Mind (Feeling). This kind of standpoint on the relation between Mind and Nature seems different from Liu Zongzhou's standpoint of "return to Nature-noumenon", and is even closer to Wang Yangming's way of thinking about the unity between Mind and Principle. However, in this respect, Huang Zongxi did not elaborate further.

From the perspective of the evolution of Mindology, the aspects that are even more worth noting in Huang Zongxi's thought are the exposition and definition of the relation between effort and noumenon, and the relation between individual and whole.

1. What Effort Attains Is Noumenon

In Huang Zongxi's view, it was not unrelated between the relation of Mind and Nature, and the relation of noumenon and effort. In the relation between Mind and Nature, Huang Zongxi affirmed that Nature could be seen in Mind and further pointed out: "Mind cannot be seen; it can only be seen in Thing." (*Ibid.* vol.2) This Mind refers usually to moral noumenon (Mind-Body); "Thing" refers to serving parents and respecting elder brothers, i.e. the practical effort in the moral domain. The intrinsic meaning of "Mind can be only seen in Thing" is that noumenon can not be separated from effort. Huang Zongxi made a distinction between true noumenon and imaginative noumenon, and held that noumenon beyond effort had only the imaginative meaning: "The noumenon without effort can only be imaginative or speculative, and is not true noumenon." (*Academic Cases of the Confucian Scholars in the Ming Dynasty*, vol.60) Wang Yangming once held the distinction between a priori noumenon and a posteriori effort as the prerequisite of the theory of attaining innate knowledge, yet in his view, the effort of attaining innate knowledge was only the means to attain noumenon, not the condition for the formation and existence of noumenon. In contrast, Huang Zongxi emphasized that no effort meant no true noumenon, and understood effort as the necessary prerequisite to make noumenon possible. Here it already demonstrated a tendency of departure from the scope of Mindology.

No effort means no true noumenon. This view emphasizes the connection of real noumenon with effort. From here, Huang Zongxi in a more universal sense defined the relation between noumenon and effort: "There is no noumenon in Mind, and what effort attains is noumenon." (Preface to *Academic Cases of the Confucian Scholars in the Ming Dynasty*) The noumenon of Mind is a transcendental presupposition of Mindology, and that there is no noumenon in Mind means a suspension of such a priori noumenon. As related previously, in content, the noumenon in opposition to effort first refers to the subject's spirit; in a broad sense, it refers in general to the comprehensive unity of the subject's consciousness. Its concrete connotations are unfolded in the different relations respectively as the basis of the cultivation of Moral Nature, internal structure of moral cognition, internal norms of moral practice, etc. In Huang Zongxi's view, spiritual noumenon was not transcendental predetermination, and it in essence took form in a posteriori course of the practice and attainment of innate knowledge, and was based on this course as its way of existence. Before Huang Zongxi, from Wang Yangming to his followers of different sects, Mindology in its course of evolution had never given up its transcendental presupposition of noumenon; the theory of return to quietude interpreted innate knowledge as a quiet and unconscious noumenon, and even expressed a mystified tendency of noumenon. Huang Zongxi's above dissolution of noumenon of Mind sublated apriority of noumenon, and at the same time avoided the mystification and solidification of noumenon.

In essence, spiritual noumenon is always in a course of constant generation, and only in the course of spiritual and practical activities can it have its reality. It is always very difficult to avoid the transcendental presupposition or the transcendental posit in the discussion of noumenon without the connection of the course of spiritual activity and practical activity. David Hume believed that there would be no self without perceptive activity, and he noticed this point in one aspect. Huang Zongxi affirmed that there was no noumenon in Mind, and what effort attained was noumenon. He also saw the same point. Huang Zongxi's view can be regarded as the logical result of the evolution of the distinction between noumenon and effort. The emphasis on the unity of noumenon and effort is the basic standpoint of Mindology. Wang Yangming already affirmed this criterion from different aspects by advocating the attainment of innate knowledge and claiming that there was no distinction at the beginning between internality and externality of noumenon. The Effort Sect of Wang Yangming's school believed that the inability to exert effort was not noumenon, and the inability to attain noumenon was not effort. This further elaborated the point concretely. The latter provided even more direct theoretical precursor for Huang Zongxi. However, whether it was

Wang Yangming or his followers, they never gave up the transcendental presupposition of noumenon; at the same time, they affirmed the attainment of noumenon through effort, and in correspondence to it was the tension between historicity of effort and non-historicity of noumenon. In contrast, Huang Zongxi defined spiritual activity as the condition of the formation and the way of existence of the spiritual noumenon, and this no doubt transcended the above tension. The latter suspended transcendental noumenon, and at the same time began to depart from the domain of Mindology.

The theory that there is no noumenon in Mind manifested in the relation between moral consciousness and moral practice concretely claims that benevolence and righteousness are conceptual while service of parents and respect of elder brothers are real: "Benevolence and righteousness are conceptual, but service for parents and respect of elder brothers are real; benevolence and righteousness cannot be seen, while service of parents and respect of elder brothers can be seen." (*On Master Meng Zi*, vol.4) Benevolence and righteousness in a broad sense are not only universal norms, but also refer to the internalized moral consciousness and internal Moral Nature of the norms. Here they mainly refers to the latter; service of parents and respect of elder brothers are moral practice. The distinction between concept and reality here first involves the formation of moral consciousness. Huang Zongxi had the following concrete explanation about it: When a man was born into this world, he would be in certain ethical relationships (for instance, family relationships between parents and children, and between younger brother and elder brother), and this is a basic ontological fact. This "inseparable relationship" refers to its establishedness; that "this is real" refers to its reality. This relation of reality gradually forms the moral practice in serving parents and respecting elder brothers. This kind of moral practice seems at first a form of conduct of spontaneity, but at the same time it embodies real effort. As the effort of moral practice evolves from comparative spontaneity to comparative consciousness, moral consciousness of benevolence, righteousness, ritual and wisdom, etc. also begins gradually to germinate and develop. Hence

"There is service of parents, then there is the name of benevolence"; "There is respect of elder brothers, then there is the name of righteousness." (*Ibid.*) In essence, when there is the effort of service of parents and respect of elder brothers, there is the noumenon of benevolence, righteousness, ritual and wisdom. The moral consciousness as the spiritual noumenon takes its form in the effort of moral practice.

Based on the above views, Huang Zongxi criticized Wang Yangming: "Yangming once said, to initiate service of father with the Mind of pure Heavenly Principle is filial piety; he does not know that what Heavenly Principle initiates from parents is benevolence."(*Five Collections of Mr. Nanlei Wending*, vol.3) To initiate service of father with the Mind of pure Heavenly Principle is based on the transcendental presupposition of noumenon as the prerequisite, and its point of emphasis lies in the function of a priori noumenon on a posteriori effort. In what Heavenly Principle initiates from parents, the real ethical relationship (relationship between parents and children) and the relevant formulated effort of moral practice are placed in a position close to the origin. Wang Yangming certainly did not deny the function of a posteriori effort in the attainment of innate knowledge, but this kind of arrival (attainment) itself must have the establishedness (apriority) of its attained object (noumenon) as the prerequisite. Because of this presupposition, it is difficult for Wang Yangming's Mindology to completely transcend the tension between noumenon and effort. Huang Zongxi's criticism of Wang Yangming indicated that he had to some extent been conscious of the problem embodied in Mindology.

The moral consciousness of benevolence, righteousness, etc. formed in the moral practice through service of parents and respect of elder brothers mainly focuses on the individual. The relation between noumenon and effort is not merely restricted to the moral practice of the individual. In a broad sense, it also refers to social activities such as state governance. Huang Zongxi criticized some of his contemporaries for "regarding the study of the Way and the service of state governance as two different ways". Here the service of state governance refers to the social application of practical knowledge for state administration, and it in essence is a social historical course. Generally speaking, the study of the Way refers to a command of universal natural laws and social norms, and the further transformation of them into the internal spiritual noumenon of the subject. Here it is worth noting that Huang Zongxi associated the course of understanding the body of the Way and the transformation of it into noumenon with the course of governance of state affairs in a broad sense, and thus extended the effort of attaining innate knowledge from moral practice of the individual to the practical activity of the species (society). As related before, when the Donglin scholars of the late Ming Dynasty stressed that "It is only conducive when learning is applied to personal practice", they already began to include the activities of governance of state affairs into the effort of attainment of innate knowledge. Huang Zongxi affirmed the unity of the study of the Way and the governance of state affairs; he doubtlessly shared some of the views with the Donglin scholars. However, Huang Zongxi emphasized more on the course of the formation of noumenon in elucidating that there was no established body of the Way from that there was no noumenon in Mind: That the study of the Way and the governance of state affairs were not two different ways means understanding effort as a historical course of species in a broad sense, and further defining spiritual noumenon in the perspective of the historical course of species.

The emphasis on the historical course was more profoundly unfolded in Huang Zongxi's study of the intellectual history and academic historiography. His position in the Chinese intellectual history was established to a great extent on the basis of his study of the intellectual and academic history. His systematic generalization and study of the intellectual history and academic history in the Song and Ming dynasties, in a sense, are pioneering. His interpretation and exposition of the relation between noumenon and effort were also based on the reflection and generalization of the intellectual history as his study background: A basic fact "There is no noumenon in Mind, and what effort attains is the noumenon" was expressed clearly in his preface to his main work of the intellectual history of *Academic Cases of the Confucian Scholars of the Ming Dynasty*.

In the perspective of the historical course of the intellectual evolution, noumenon refers to the state of human spiritual development and the result of human knowledge expressed in the form of truth. "No noumenon in Mind" in this sense means that the state of human spiritual development and the result of human knowledge expressed in the form of truth do not possess a priori and predetermined attribute. That what effort attains is noumenon emphasizes that this spiritual form and cognitive result of knowledge are formed in the course of cognitive development of the species. Of course, the form of human spiritual development and cognitive result are not abstract, and they always accumulate and develop through the concrete exploration of different ages. With regard to the Ming Dynasty, the development of cultural spirit was gradually reflected through the research efforts of the thinkers: "To become an expert after exhaustive exploration of all possible differences in Mind." (Preface to *Academic Cases of the Confucian Scholars in the Ming Dynasty*) It is the different explorations of the thinkers that constitute the history of development of human spirit. Here, effort is concretely demonstrated as a course of cognitive development of the species.

For a study of the cognitive history of the species from the view of "What effort attains is noumenon", special attention should be paid to the creative interpretations of different thinkers. In the Guide to *Academic Cases of the Confucian Scholars of the Ming Dynasty*, Huang Zongxi pointed out: "As for the way of learning and inquiring, each one's unique views are genuine." Each one's unique views are the unique understandings through creative exploration. With this as the prerequisite, Huang Zongxi further affirmed the diversity of academic study and orientations of intellectual development: "Their ways have to be diversified." (Preface to *Academic Cases of the Confucian Scholars of the Ming Dynasty*) In regard to the relation between noumenon and effort, the affirmation here is that the formation and unfoldment of noumenon cannot be separated from effort. As for the relation between individualistic principle and universalistic principle, it again expresses the emphasis of individualistic principle.

Of course, the genuineness of each one's unique views and the affirmation of the diversity of intellectual explorations do not mean rejecting a command of the body of the Way in favor of the different ways of effort. In the light of spiritual development of the species, noumenon embodies not only the exploration in different ways, but also internal unity. Huang Zongxi generalized the relation of the two as "one noumenon with all possible different ways": One noumenon is the spiritual noumenon (cognitive result of the species in expression of truth) with the body of the Way as its substance, and all possible different ways mean the unique explorations in different times of different thinkers. On one hand, the spiritual noumenon of the species takes form and exists in all possible efforts of exploration, so even a prejudice and an opposite view should be paid attention to; on the other hand, all possible different ways constitute the different aspects of the universal noumenon, just as all rivers return to the sea. In essence, between the unified spiritual noumenon and the diversified efforts of exploration do not exist tension and confrontation. This kind of understanding of human spiritual phenomenon, to a great extent, has already connected the relation between individuality and universality, and the relation between noumenon and effort embedded in the distinction between Mind and Nature: It not only represents the tendency of unity between noumenon and effort, but also makes a dual affirmation of individualistic principle and universalistic principle from the perspective of the formation and development of spiritual noumenon. This orientation of the logic evolution of Huang Zongxi's thought in a sense seemed to return to the internal theme of Wang Yangming's Mindology. Of course, behind this return exist profound differences between their philosophical standpoints.

2. Distinction between the Individual and the Whole

Before Huang Zongxi, Li Zhi put forth his proposition that "Heaven gives birth to a man, and he will certainly be useful in his own way", and criticized the various aspects of the orthodox values through the stress on the value of individual. Li Zhi's heresy was based on the theory of Child-Mind as his theoretic prerequisite, while the theory of Child-Mind is established on the extraction of universal Heavenly Principle from innate knowledge. In this sense, Li Zhi's denial of the orthodox values can also be regarded as the reformation of Wang Yangming's Mindology. After Li Zhi, Huang Zongxi rethought about the relations between the individual and the whole, monarch and people in the world, etc., and further broke through the scope of Wang Yangming's Mindology.

A new historical phenomenon at the turn of the Ming and Qing Dynasties was the growth of commercial economy and capitalism. This kind of new social economic factors also left its historical impressions in the theory of Huang Zongxi. Huang Zongxi voiced his dissent on the traditional views of depreciating industry and commerce: "The worldly Confucian scholars do not make any investigation, and they believe industry and commerce are unimportant and talk wantonly to depreciate it." (*Records in Waiting for a Visit in Darkness*) In opposition to the worldly Confucian scholars, Huang Zongxi emphasized that industry and commerce were both important. Therefore, the urban residents engaging in business and industry demanded to break through the restrictions of feudal systems, wished to promote the development of industry and commerce, and put forward the relevant concepts — all these should be logically reasonable. This kind of view has transcended Wang Yangming's prejudice against fame and wealth, and is close to Li Zhi's thought. However, Huang Zongxi affirmed the positions of industry and commerce in consideration of their function in the whole social life, and the ideas of urban residents that he expressed was considerably self-conscious in nature.

Starting from the above views, Huang Zongxi studied Nature of Man: "From the beginning of Man, everyone is selfish, and everyone seeks self-interest." (*Ibid.*) The view that selfism is Nature shares similarity with Li Zhi's theory. However, Li Zhi mainly regarded selfism as the innate nature of the individual, while what Huang Zongxi said "from the beginning of Man" means the historical origin of human beings. Thus, selfism is the Nature of Man as a whole. According to Huang Zongxi's view, the injustice of monarchical despotism lay in the denial of the selfish right of all the people under heaven: Monarchs in the world often held the interests of the world as their own, and left all harms to others; therefore, under their power, the people under heaven didn't dare to be selfish or seek self interest. "If there is no monarch, everyone can be selfish, and everyone can seek his own interests." (*Ibid.*) The people under heaven are the sum of individuals. Affirmation of the just cause of selfishness and self-interest means admitting that every subject has the right to pursue and defend his own interests.

It is worth noting that Huang Zongxi's view did not generalize selfism and self-interests narrowly as personal interests, but interpreted it in a broad sense as the interests of every individual. Here it demonstrates a tendency to unite individual interests with the interests of a community (people under heaven as the sum of individuals): It is not difficult to see this point in the connection between "selfism and self-interest" and "all can obtain them". Before Huang Zongxi, Wang Yangming affirmed the unity between individuality and universality through giving innate knowledge a dual character of Mind and Principle. It is from this prerequisite that Wang Yangming noticed the role of morality when he advocated the regulation of individual's conduct with universal Principle; conduct should come from the individual's internal will, and in that sense his view was different from that of Chengs-Zhu who rejected the individual's will in favor of universal Principle one-sidedly. However, besides the relation between self and community, Wang Yangming again put forward the concept of "non-self", and demanded that the individual should unconditionally submit to the whole with monarch as the symbol. Different from Wang Yangming, Li Zhi denied the restriction of despotism in favor of individualistic principle, and at the same time displayed a tendency of neglecting the interests of community and regarded selfishness and self-interests as the first principle. This was obviously a prejudiced theory.

Huang Zongxi's understanding of the relation between individual interests and interests of people under heaven is undoubtedly influenced by Wang Yangming's unity of individualistic principle and universalistic principle, but there also exists an important difference between the two.

Disagreeing from Wang Yangming's conclusion of the whole as despotism and hierarchically patriarchal relation, Huang Zongxi understood the whole as mainly the people under heaven, i.e. community as the total of individuals. At the same time, in Huang Zongxi's view, the unity of individual (self) and community (people under heaven) did not mean the annexation of the individual into the community as the prerequisite, but was based on the full realization of the individual's interests. This kind of view has more or less departed from the feudal orthodox ideology, and in some aspect it is close to the modern distinction between self and community. It is not only different from Wang Yangming's concept of "non-self", but also different from Li Zhi's over-emphasis on the individualistic principle.

Certainly, Huang Zongxi's view is not merely the result of speculation and deduction of the relation between individuality and universality, and it has also the profound historical causes. At the turn of the Ming and Qing Dynasties, besides the development of commercial economy and some changes in the social economic relations, an important historical phenomenon is the striking ethnical conflicts. In 1644, the Qing army broke into the Ming passes, and what ensued was the cruel racial oppression, which naturally met resistance of the peoples of different nationalities within the passes. It is the struggles against the ethnical oppression that the interests of the whole could be accorded serious attention. Huang Zongxi once assembled soldiers to fight against the Qing army and had a personal experience about it, while Li Zhi had never had such experience. While Huang Zongxi's affirmation of the rationality of self-interest mainly expressed the ideas of urban residents related to commercial economy, the connection between self-interest and people under heaven in a certain sense reflected the historical demand of resisting national oppression; the former enabled Huang Zongxi to transcend Wang Yangming's horizons, and the latter to a certain extent caused Huang Zongxi to avoid Li Zhi's one-sidedness.

With the prerequisite of affirming every man could be selfish and seek self-interest, Huang Zongxi made the following definition for the function of monarch: The purpose of establishing a monarch was for the governance of the country, while the concrete content for the governance of the country was to enable all people under heaven to obtain their interests. According to Huang Zongxi's understanding, a monarch himself was only "one self", for he had no supreme quality to surpass all people under heaven. On the contrary, he should commit himself to following the will of people under heaven. It is based on this view that Huang Zongxi advocated that serving an official position (as an official) was not for one monarch himself (or a family), but for all the people throughout the country.

Huang Zongxi's view expressed at the turn of the Ming and Qing Dynasties is without doubt a a groundbreaking idea in the Chinese Middle Ages, as it aroused responses of many contemporary and later thinkers. It is not difficult to see this point from Tang Zhen, a philosopher at the beginning of the Qing Dynasty, who was also influenced in philosophy by Wang Yangming's theory of innate knowledge. In his view, innate knowledge at first was the individual's consciousness within the subject: "Innate knowledge is within me." (*The Book of Retreat*) From the affirmation of individualistic principle, Tang Zhen advocated "love of one's body first", and this view paid great attention to the sensitive existence of the individual. However, in emphasizing individualistic principle, Tang Zhen at the same time demanded "no harm to others", i.e. he opposed the unconditional rejection of others' interests. In Tang Zhen's view, the ideal principle was "Benefit oneself, and do no harm to others." (*Ibid.*) Here, the relation between self and others is mutually compatible: The pursuit of the individual's interests (beneficial to self) does not mean the rejection of other's interests (do no harm to others). With regard to the intention to coordinate individual interests with community interests, this view is obviously close to that of Huang Zongxi.

Wang Yangming incorporated individualistic principle and universal principle with the proposition that Mind was Principle, and expressed the tendency of uniting universality and individuality in the domain of Mind and Nature. The Taizhou Sect, Li Zhi, etc. made elaborations on individualistic principle from multiple aspects, and Liu Zongzhou reemphasized universalistic principle; it seems that Huang Zongxi and Tang Zhen returned to the starting point of Mindology. Of course, this is a kind of return at a higher level: Huang Zongxi, Tang Zhen, etc. affirmed the unity of individuality and universality, and they transcended the domain of Mind and Nature. Their thought possessed even more profound historical connotations.

Chapter Five

Reverberations of Mindology in the Modern Times

When the social turbulence at the turn of the Ming and Qing Dynasties quieted down, Chengs-Zhu's Principlism once again was posited as the orthodox ideology, and the rise of the Plain Learning constituted a different scenario of the academic study of the Qing Dynasty. With the exclusive dominance of Zhu Xi's Principlism, the transcendental Heavenly Principle once again overwhelmed innate knowledge of the subject, and the positivism of the Plain Learning dissolved the basis of Mind-Body: Mindology was cast aside historically. However, after the silence for a long time in the Qing Dynasty, Wang Yangming's Mindology in the modern times had a renaissance. It intertwined with different trends of the western thought introduced to the east, and produced a rather complex influence in the modern China.

1.　Innate Knowledge and Individuality

Wang Yangming united individual Mind and universal Principle with innate knowledge, which embodied the emphasis on individualistic principle. After the Chinese society entered the modern times, the promotion of individuality became a demand of the times with the development of ideological enlightenment. The early enlightenment thinkers introduced the western thought about the emancipation of individuality, etc., and at the same time, they tried unswervingly to search in the traditional thought for the theoretical basis to break through the despotic system. Wang Yangming's Mindology was thus highly recommended for its affirmation of individualistic principle. In contrast to the esteem of Wang Yangming's Mindology, Chengs-Zhu's Principlism that emphasized the universal Heavenly Principle was rejected. Without doubt, behind the identity with Mind-Body and the rejection of Heavenly Principle is a certain historical choice.

Since the Song Dynasty, the orthodox Principlism with Chengs-Zhu as representatives generalized Heavenly Principle as the absolute mandate, and the moral laws as the incarnation of Heavenly Principle also gradually became a tool of restriction on man. In the modern times, the shadow of Heavenly Principle did not disappear. Kang Youwei[1] once wrote the following conclusion about this kind of phenomenon: "Nowadays people only wanted to restrain others with the moral principles of the Confucian scholars of the Song Dynasty." Here the Confucian scholars of the Song Dynasty refer to the Principlists in Chengs-Zhu's school. Modern thinkers such as Kang Youwei were discontented with the oppression of Heavenly Principle. They repeatedly criticized that Zhu Xi was prejudiced to stress ascesis with righteousness, and even to sever people's feelings, while in fact, "People's feelings indeed cannot be severed." (*Elucidation on Meng Zi*, vol.4) Feelings here refer to man's will and emotions, while "righteousness" means universal norms. Severance of people's feelings means repression and rejection of man's internal will with universal norms. This criticism already took into consideration the historical limitation of the orthodox Principlism, which neglected the fact that moral conduct should be based on the internal will of the subject and is doubtlessly in conformity in theory with Wang Yangming's refusal to reject Mind of Man in favor of Mind of the Way. Kang Youwei's student Liang Qichao[2] clearly associated the criticisms of Chengs-Zhu with the recognition of Mindology. He once compared Wang Yangming's thought with Chengs-Zhu's philosophy,

---

[1] Kang Youwei (1848 – 1927), a political thinker, reformist and calligrapher of the late Qing Dynasty. He led movements to establish a constitutional monarchy in 1898 but failed.

[2] Liang Qichao (1873 – 1929), a journalist, philosopher, and reformist in the late Qing Dynasty, who inspired Chinese scholars with his writings and reform movements. He organized reforms with Kang Youwei in 1898.

and held that Wang Yangming's thought was "closer to the original Confucianism, and better than the philosophy of Chengs-Zhu". (*Confucian Philosophy*)

Although Wang Yangming did not agree with Chengs-Zhu on the opposition between Heavenly Principle and the will of the subject, he never doubted about the traditional cardinal guides and constant virtues, and name-reality doctrine as the incarnation of Heavenly Principle. On the contrary, the modern thinkers opposed the oppression on the will of the subject by Heavenly Principle, and further pointed their criticism at the moral system of the three cardinal guides and five constant virtues itself. Tan Sitong[①] held that the five traditional ethical relationships "oppress coercively natural pleasure, and force man to lose all rights of independence." (*Complete Collection of Tan Sitong*, 198) The moral norms in the form of Heavenly Principle often are concretized as cardinal guides, constant virtues, and name-reality doctrines, whose restrictions underlie the oppression of Heavenly Principle. This system of cardinal guides and constant virtues strangles the subject's internal will (natural pleasure), and at the same time deprives the subject of his right of independence with external restrictions. As a kind of right, the demand of independence has already surpassed the relation of morality, and involves in a broad sense the social political domain. It is a course of profound transformation of concepts from emphasizing the voluntariness in morality to rejecting the traditional cardinal guides, constant virtues and name-reality doctrines and demanding the independent rights of the subject. It is not only somewhat intellectually connected with the influence of Mindology, but also possesses some historical substance that Mind is unable to include.

In accordance with the stress on voluntariness and independence, the modern thinkers put forward the demand of freedom. Liang Qichao pointed out: "Freedom is the universally acknowledged truth. It is a necessity in life, and can be applied everywhere." (*On the New People*) This

---

① Tan Sitong (1865 – 1898), a thinker and reformist in the late Qing Dynasty. He was executed at the age of 33 when the Hundred Days' Reform failed.

kind of freedom first refers to free choice in moral conduct. In theory, affirming that conduct comes from the internal will of the subject means acknowledging that the subject has free choice in his conduct. This relation Wang Yangming had already noticed, and his followers further studied it from different aspects. This theory in Wang Yangming's Mindology became important traditional resources for the modern thinkers in elaborating the concept of freedom. Liang Qichao believed that his "theory of new people" about free personality was the "focal elaboration on the thoughts of Wang Yangming and his followers". Of course, Wang Yangming talked about the relation between moral conduct and free choice, but he did not give any further theoretic analysis about it. Liang Qichao absorbed some relevant theories from the modern western thinkers, and made comparatively systematic analysis of the relation and expressed it in the modern form.

Because of emphasis on the moral freedom, the modern thinkers paid great attention to the independence of personality. Liang Qichao held: "Today talking about independence, we should first talk about independence of individual." (*Ten Moral Natures in Opposition and Complementarity*) Individual independence refers not only to political emancipation from despotic control, but also to full promotion of individuality. This kind of independent individual is usually understood as an extraordinary man. In Liang Qichao's view, the characteristic of an extraordinary man lay in that "He comes and goes alone in the world, and can create the world trend alone." As related previously, Wang Yangming once recommended the rise of a man with no expectation as the quality of an extraordinary man, although Wang Yangming's non-expectation referred to keeping above worldly consideration mainly through moral cultivation in order to attain the realm of inner sagehood, and did not include the meaning of freedom from restrictions of cardinal guides and constant virtues. However, if the demand of non-expectation is further extended, it can also obtain new connotations. In fact, it is from here that Li Zhi put forth his theory of non-patronization. Likewise, Liang Qichao's thought also has inseparable historical connection with Wang Yangming's Mindology. Of course, it is not a simple inheritance of Mindology: What

Wang Yangming pursued is the personality of internal sagehood, and what Liang Qichao aspired for is the free personality with full development of individuality of the modern society.

One of the characteristics for free personality is the ability of independent thinking. In Liang Qichao's words, "I have ears and eyes, and I investigate my world with them; I have a mind and can think, and I will exhaust my principles." That is, "Whether it is observation or judgment, I cannot depend on external views, and should rely on my own thinking as the final criterion." This view was obviously influenced by Wang Yangming's theory of innate knowledge as the standard: At the point of affirming that the subject had the ability to pass judgment on right and wrong, the two share a line of inheritance. As a matter of fact, Liang Qichao indeed paid great attention to Wang Yangming's theory of innate knowledge as the standard, and highly recommended it. Once he praised it as "a pertinent remark". (*On the New People*) Of course, with regard to the modern thinkers, such as Liang Qichao, etc., individual independent thinking is significant in that it helps to counter the arbitrary interpretation in the study of Confucian classics, and this obviously is different from Wang Yangming's standpoint which never departed from the study of Confucian classics.

Free development of personality is the historical demand of the modern trend of enlightenment. In comparison with this demand, there is a duality of Wang Yangming's Mindology: For one thing, Mindology itself did not attain the level of modern concepts, such as freedom of individuality, etc.; for another, it stressed the individual's will, affirmed the principle of independence in moral conduct, approved of the function of the individual in the judgment of right and wrong, and good and evil, and also provided important materials of thinking for modern thinkers. Thus, when modern Chinese thinkers, after their preliminary contact with the modern western humanism, tried to find a traditional basis for the modern enlightenment, it is quite natural that they paid attention to Wang Yangming's Mindology. It is the need of the times that gave Mindology the modern prominence that Chengs-Zhu's Principlism could not hope to attain.

2. Innate Knowledge and Intuition

Holding different views from Kang Youwei, Tan Sitong, Liang Qichao, etc., who mainly associated the principle of individuality in Wang Yangming's Mindology with modern demands such as freedom of individuality, Liang Shuming[①] especially made elaboration on it from the perspective of individual consciousness. Liang Shuming was an important philosopher before and after the May Fourth Movement in 1919, and his theory is characterized by a combination of Confucianism, Buddhism, and the philosophies of Bergson and Schopenhauer, etc. In the traditional Confucianism, what Liang Shuming held in foremost esteem is Wang Yangming's Mindology.

Liang Shuming paid special attention to the concept of innate knowledge in Wang Yangming's Mindology. Wang Yangming understood innate knowledge as the unity of individual Mind and universal Principle, and the Principle also included Principlist thinking. Thus, the unity of Mind and Principle means the affirmation of the restriction of Principlism on the individual's consciousness. Differing from Wang Yangming, Liang Shuming affirmed Wang Yangming's theory of innate knowledge, but at the same time extracted the universal Principle embedded in it. He thought that "no functions of concept and reason were innate knowledge". Once the universal Principle (reason) was extracted, innate knowledge would be equal to pure individual consciousness. In this sense, innate knowledge, in Liang Shuming's view, was intuition: "With the rise of Master Yangming in the Ming Dynasty, he began to eliminate the malpractice of exhaustive investigation of Principle externally, and return to intuition — to call it innate knowledge." (*The East and West Cultures and Their Philosophies*) What this interpretation stressed is mainly the definition of individuality in innate knowledge.

In connecting innate knowledge with intuition, Wang Yangming at the same time further defined the connotation of intuition. In Liang

---

① Liang Shuming (1893 – 1988), an important modern philosopher, educator, and social activist. He wrote influential books on culture and philosophy, and led the Rural Reconstruction Movement.

Shuming's view, intuition was characteristic in that it was first of all "difficult to explain to others in language", i.e. there was no way of expression and communication with others in the language of concepts. Intuition took place only in an instant; once it happened, it could only exist in the way of intuition, and "could not exist in the form of reason". That is, what was obtained through intuition could not be forever solidified in the form of universal rationality. Here, Liang Shuming actually regarded intuition as individual experience isolated from rationality. In the perspective of the development of Principlism, Lu Jiuyuan usually understood "Mind" as purely individual consciousness: When he regarded Mind as "my Mind", it means that he only provided Mind with the definition of the individual, but Wang Yangming's theory of innate knowledge paid attention to the unity of individuality and universality in the subject's consciousness through the connection between Mind and Principle. It seems that Liang Shuming's above view started from Wang Yangming's Mindology and again returned to Lu Jiuyuan's theory.

After reason was extracted from intuition, Liang Shuming further adopted a depreciative attitude towards it. In his view, the universe was an indivisible whole. Intuition could command this unity of the universe better, while reason often divided it and made it difficult to combine into one again. This view originated from Bergson, who held that in tuition, "I" and all things of creation were in mixed unison, while rationality more often divided this unity. Like Bergson, Liang Shuming's understanding of the function of rationality is obviously prejudiced. In fact, the way of rationality is both analytical and synthetic. Wang Yangming, to some extent, noticed this similar point, and he repeatedly emphasized not only "distinction" but also the unity of learning and effort. He clearly demonstrated the point. It is based on this understanding that Wang Yangming always affirmed the function of reason. Liang Shuming held that reason only functioned in "division", thus he expressed his negative attitude. This, more or less, deviated from Wang Yangming's standpoint of rationality.

It can be seen that Liang Shuming intensified Wang Yangming's definition of individuality in innate knowledge, and at the same time, he extracted universal reason out of innate knowledge; therefore, he equated innate knowledge to intuition. In contrast with the modern thinkers such as Kang Youwei, who identified themselves with Wang Yangming's Mindology from the perspective of rational enlightenment, Liang Shuming seemed to have led Mindology to irrationality through the transformation of innate knowledge into intuition.

3. Mind-Power and Will-Desire

One salient phenomenon in the modern Chinese intellectual history is the rise of voluntarism. From Gong Zizheng to Tan Sitong, Liang Qichao, Zhang Taiyan[1], etc., all displayed their voluntaristic tendency to various degrees. During the May Fourth Movement in 1919, Liang Shuming even established a relatively complete system of voluntarism. It can be said that in modern China, voluntarism already became an important trend of thought. The appearance of this trend had its profound social and historical origins, and at the same time was restrained by the modern western voluntarism and traditional thought. Because of the emphasis on the functions of Mind-Body and Will, Wang Yangming's Mindology (including the thought of the Taizhou Sect) had a prominent influence on the modern thinkers who focused on Mind-Power and Will-Desire.

The focus on the self was a popular characteristic of the early voluntarists in the modern times, and it first appeared in Gong Zizhen's works. In contrast to the traditional theory of heavenly mandate, Gong Zizhen elevated the self to the supreme position: "The ruler of all people is not the Way, nor the ultimate, but is called I myself." "I" was not only the ruler of all people, but also the determiner of heaven, earth and all things of creation. That "My strength can create mountains and rivers" and "My vital energy can create heaven and earth" demonstrate this point

---

[1] Zhang Taiyan (1868 – 1936), an outstanding philologist, philosopher, and textual critic, known for his outspoken support for the revolution at the end of the Qing Dynasty.

vividly. This kind of view to regard the self as the first principle obviously shares some similarity in theory with the view of the Taizhou Sect that "I can shape and guide life". As for Gong Zizhen, the strength of the self was concentrated in the power of Mind ("all in the power of Mind"). After Gong Zizhen, Kang Youwei and other thinkers in the same way elevated the power of Mind to an important position.

Self-reliance and self-establishment were the historical demands of the modern thinkers of enlightenment. In the perspective of social evolution, they represented the struggle for salvation and self-empowerment. With regard to the relation between self and history, it means the advocacy of the strength of the self. Tan Sitong held that independence and self-empowerment should not rely on the external force, but should be based on the self. It is because of this view that Tan Sitong advocated "to seek self-empowerment through the self". This view was in conformity with the theory of "to seek self-reliance" of the Taizhou Sect. Of course, in Tan Sitong's view, the "self" was mainly expressed as a force of self-empowerment, which referred mainly to the national independence and prosperity; for that reason, Tan Sitong's view of seeking self-reliance has a historical meaning that is different from that of the Taizhou Sect.

In Tan Sitong's theory, the strength of the self was first connected with Mind-Power. In his view, the strength of the self in the end originated from the power of Mind. Without Mind-Power, Man could do nothing. Concretely, Mind-Power had dual characteristics: One was self-reliance, i.e. no external force could control it; the second was single-mindedness, i.e. no external force could change its orientation. The two aspects roughly constituted the quality of Will. From Wang Yangming's Mind-Body to Tan Sitong's power of Mind, the function of Mind was often led to the transformation of reality. In fact, what Tan Sitong repeatedly emphasized is the reformation of reality with Mind-Power: "Even heaven and earth cannot be compared with Mind-Power. Although heaven and earth are vast and extensive, it can be created, destroyed and transformed with Mind-Power, all to desired effects." To transform heaven and earth with Mind-Power is of course an unlimited exaggeration of the function of Will, but at the same time it also reflects the progressive intention of trying every means to create a new historical era.

Differing from Tan Sitong who advocated self-reliance and self-establishment and emphasized self-support, Liang Qichao associated freedom with strong power. In Liang Qichao's view, the realization of freedom could not be separated from strong power: "In the world there is no other force than strong power." (*On Freedom*) The strong power here is different from hegemony in politics, but is mainly willpower against external force, i.e. "fight against other force of hindrance to obtain what oneself desires". As a means of fighting against external force to realize freedom, strong power is always connected with the subject's resolution and tenacity. In Liang Qichao's view, this was the forte of Wang Yangming's Mindology. He repeatedly praised "impassionate and tenacious efforts in Wang Yangming's philosophy", and believed that "The morale in the late Ming Dynasty is unprecedented, because the contribution of Wang Yangming's philosophy is on a par with the Great Yu of the Xia Dynasty." (*On the New People*) The morale of "impassionate and tenacious efforts" mainly demonstrated the dimension of Will. It is not difficult to see here the connection between the thought of the modern thinkers focusing on the function of Will and Wang Yangming's philosophy.

How can one fight against other forces through self-empowerment? Liang Qichao in the same way introduced the concept of Mind-Power, and held that everything in the world "can be accomplished with Mind-Power of a perfect man." Liang Qichao emphasized power of mind, and undoubtedly shared similar views with Tan Sitong. However, their focuses seemed somewhat different. In comparison with Tan Sitong who stressed on the self-reliance of Mind-Power, Liang Qichao emphasized the tenacity of Mind-Power. In Liang Qichao's view, success from Mind-Power was just success from tenacity: "He who has tenacity will succeed, and he will fail otherwise." The difference on Mind-Power between Tan Sitong and Liang Qichao had not only historical origins, but also theoretical causes. With regard to the historical background, Liang Qichao's systematic elaboration of Mind-Power mainly took place after the Reform Movement of 1898. Before it, the main problem the reformists faced was the historical selection (reform or not reform), while after the failure of the reform, when facing the serious frustration, the problem of how to stimulate the morale of the reformists with willpower became a pressing one, and Liang Qichao's emphasis on the tenacity of will in a sense reflected this historical character.

Almost at the same time to embrace voluntarism as Liang Qichao was Zhang Taiyan. Zhang Taiyan did not agree with Tan Sitong and Liang Qichao on the reformism in politics, but they shared the similar views in the emphasis of will. With regard to the theoretic origin, Zhang Taiyan's affinity to voluntarism was subtly connected to the influence of Wang Yangming's Mindology in a similar manner. He once generalized the theoretic value of Wang Yangming's philosophy as follows: "What are the fortes of Wang's philosophy? Only self-esteem and courage." (*In Reply to Tie Zheng*) Self-esteem is self-affirmation, and courage is tenacity of will. In Zhang Taiyan's view, Wang Yangming himself represented the tenacious quality of will honestly: He was respectable, for he had "courage to do of his own free will". The point in his remark was of course not the evaluation of Wang Yangming himself, but the association of Mindology with the will of the subject.

In correspondence to the commendation of Wang Yangming's "courage to do of his own free will", Zhang Taiyan held that a man was born with an independent quality and did not exist for others. There was no transcendental dominator above man. "I" certainly should treat others with humanity, but this should not "be restricted with heteronomy". That is, the subject's conduct should not be the result of regulation and compulsion. With this as the prerequisite, Zhang Taiyan further advocated "dependence on self and independence of others". Self-dependence refers to the self as the basis of conduct and reflects the esteem of the subject's strength; independence of others includes a dual meaning: "I" should not passively submit to other regulations (external norms), and "I" can choose something other than the external laws as the basis of my function. In a word, the conduct of the self should be neither restricted with social norms nor determined by external laws. This view indeed has an obvious quality of voluntarism.

It can be seen that Tan Sitong, Liang Qichao, Zhang Taiyan, etc. mainly emphasized the function of Mind-Power in the relation between the power of Mind (self Mind) and external power (other power) , and did not put will and reason in opposition. In the same way the above thinkers of the modern times embraced voluntarism under Wang Yangming's influence, their views about the relation between will and reason were more or less influenced by Wang Yangming's philosophy. In the perspective of the evolution of the theory, Wang Yangming in affirming the function of will did not deny the restriction of reason on will, but the Taizhou Sect elaborated one-sidedly from the relations between will and Principle of necessity, and between will and reason, the latter focusing on the two propositions of "I shape and guide Fate" and "Idea is the dominator of Mind". "I shape and guide Fate" is a significant argument against fatalism, and "Idea is the dominator of Mind" expresses an irrational tendency. In modern China, the thinkers who demanded reformation faced double tasks: salvation of the country and struggle for strength, and intellectual enlightenment. While the urgency of salvation of the country and struggle for strength made the modern thinkers stress the function of will and draw conclusions such as "I shape and guide the fate", the mission of intellectual enlightenment made it difficult for them to accept the irrational proposition of "Idea is the dominator of Mind"; therefore, they inclined toward the original philosophy of Wang Yangming which affirmed the function of reason.

During the May 4th Movement in 1919, it was Liang Shuming who further elucidated voluntarism. When Liang Shuming reviewed Wang Yangming's Mindology, he specially favoured the Taizhou Sect. He once said: "Only the Wang father and son of Taizhou, Mr. Xinzhai, and Mr. Dongya of the late Ming Dynasty, I like the most." Differing from Tan Sitong and others who inherited the theory of "I shape and guide Fate" of the Taizhou Sect mainly in the relation between Mind-Power and external force, Liang Shuming mainly elaborated the theory of "Idea is the dominator of Mind" in the relation between will and reason.

Liang Shuming first connected the voluntarism of the Taizhou Sect with that of Schopenhauer, and elevated intention as the first principle of the universe. In Liang Shuming's view, Man's conduct was not determined by knowledge: "Conduct comes out of Feeling and Idea." This view is doubtlessly inherited from "conduct in accordance with Idea" advocated by the Taizhou Sect. The claim that conduct is motivated by Will-Desire while knowledge has no role in the process implies the separation between reason and will, while conduct motivated by Will-Desire beyond reason is usually manifested as an irrational impulse. In the same vein as the Taizhou Sect, this view of Liang Shuming bears the tint of irrationalism to some extent.

Starting from the abovementioned view, Liang Shuming reinterpreted the concept of "rationality". In his view, rationality mainly represented the aspect of Feeling and Idea of human Mind, and it was characteristic in that it made no deduction or analysis and was manifested as an intention of love of good and hatred of evil. This view in fact interpreted rationality with voluntarism. As a special form of will, "rationality" not only went beyond the restriction of reason, but also constituted the basis of reason: The former was the fundamental, and the latter the incidental. Here, will is not only isolated from reason, but also defined as the dominator of reason.

Liang Shuming's above argument can be regarded as his elaboration on Wang Yangming's theory, especially the theory of the Taizhou Sect. In Liang Shuming's own elucidation, it is not difficult for us to see the point: "Wang's philosophy emphasized innate knowledge and advocated action. Innate knowledge does not need a posteriori knowledge, and effort brings sobriety." (*Gists of the Chinese Culture*) Wang's philosophy here mainly refers to Wang's philosophy of the Taizhou Sect. Similar to the Taizhou Sect, Liang Shuming made voluntaristic elaboration on Wang Yangming's innate knowledge, and putting knowledge and action in opposition proved this point. Action was further attributed to the application of the intention of love of good and hatred of evil. This kind of view with love and hatred as the motive of action is to some extent in conformity with the tendency of "unrestrained passion" of the Taizhou Sect.

From Tan Sitong and others who created heaven and earth with Mind-Power, to Liang Shuming who dominated reason with Will-Desire, the propositions of the Taizhou Sect that "I shape and guide Fate" and "Idea is the dominator of Mind" seemed to be unfolded in duality logically; of course, the latter displayed even stronger irrationality. The modern voluntarism is undoubtedly one-sided in theory, but in the perspective of Chinese intellectual history, the traditional philosophy on the whole lacked the in-depth study of will, which had influence on the cultivation of ideal personality, i.e. comparative ignorance of the voluntary principle. Liang Shuming succeeded Tan Sitong and others in making an even more systematic analysis of the different parts of will. Without doubt, this has the theoretical significance for further sorting out the relations between the rational consciousness and the will of the subject, etc. in the cultivation of ideal personality.

4. Unity of Knowledge and Action, and Oneness of Nature and Cultivation

The relation between knowledge and action was one of the central issues in modern Chinese philosophical discussions. Wang Yangming's theory of knowledge and action provided the modern philosophers with the resources of the traditional thought for solving the problem of distinction between knowledge and action from one aspect. In Xiong Shili's theory of oneness of Nature and cultivation, it is not difficult to see the influence of Wang Yangming's theory of knowledge and action. Xiong Shili is an important figure of New Confucianism in the modern times. Although he absorbed many ideas from Buddhism, his thought was mainly based on Confucianism. And in Confucianism, Xiong Shili especially respected Wang Yangming. He repeatedly pointed out: "Yangming's philosophy is indeed the orthodox line of Confucianism", "Of all Confucian sects, only Yangming inherited properly the thoughts of Kong Zi and Meng Zi." (*Important Quotations from Xiong Shili*) With regard to the theoretical substance, Wang Yangming's Mindology indeed constitutes an important source of Xiong Shili's philosophical system.

Wang Yangming established his theory of attainment of innate knowledge as the basis of his philosophy, while attainment of innate knowledge was again unfolded concretely as the unity of knowledge (innate knowledge) and action (effort to attain innate knowledge). According to Wang Yangming, knowledge in a broad sense includes moral consciousness. Therefore, the relation between knowledge and action is internally connected with the course of moral cultivation. As expressed in the proposition of the attainment of innate knowledge, the affirmation of the unity of a priori knowledge and a posteriori attainment constitutes an important character of Wang Yangming's Mindology. Xiong Shili on the whole accepted Wang Yangming's line of thought in his study of the relation between moral noumenon and effort of cultivation. In his view, a man certainly had transcendental Nature (transcendental moral consciousness), but this Nature could reveal itself only after a posteriori cultivation and learning, as stressed in "a desire to understand the natural Mind entails an emphasis on cultivation and learning". The focus here is the unity of heavenly bestowed Nature and a posteriori cultivation and learning, which an be summed up as "oneness of Nature and cultivation". This point of view can be regarded as the extension of Wang Yangming's theory of attainment of innate knowledge.

Nevertheless, in affirming Wang Yangming's theory of attainment of innate knowledge, Xiong Shili also absorbed some thought from Wang Fuzhi, and put forward the view that "The transcendental Nature can accomplish nothing without Man's effort", i.e. transcendental Nature cannot be transformed from latent ability into reality without a posteriori effort of Man. Here the function of Man (the subject's own effort) is not only the condition to attain transcendental Moral Nature, but also constitutes the prerequisite for the transcendental Nature to obtain the real state. It is right from this point that Xiong Shili disagreed with Wang Yangming's theory of innate knowledge, and thought "the term of innate knowledge seemingly stresses transcendence" while in fact heavenly Nature itself was also "created by Man". Fundamentally speaking, Wang Yangming's theory of attainment of innate knowledge was not separated from the theory of return to Nature.

It had certainly noted that transcendental knowledge could become the subject's self-consciousness only through a posteriori effort, but this course of attainment of innate knowledge at the same time was understood as a course of return to the transcendental Nature. Holding a somewhat different view, Xiong Shili regarded oneness of Nature and cultivation as the unity of transcendental Nature and perfection of Nature, and stressed the return from the starting point of transcendental Nature, which was at the same time a new course of generation.

Perfection of Nature as a course of constant creation and progress cannot be separated from the function of Will. The function of Will is primarily to overcome the worldly influence for the purpose of creating a new moral consciousness. Generally speaking, Principlists usually regarded worldly influence as a negative factor, and believed it had a completely negative effect on the original Nature. It is based on this view that they often took a posteriori effort as a constant course of "decrease". Starting from the view of the creation of Nature, Xiong Shili regarded the worldly custom as a dynamic force for the perfection of Nature, and believed the condition to make the worldly custom as dynamic force was to establish the true Will. Here, Xiong Shili in fact combined the course of the perfection of Nature with the restriction of Will.

The function of Will throughout the entire course of the cultivation of Nature does not demonstrate itself as a blind impulsion. Xiong Shili criticized the modern voluntarists and thought they either blindly emphasized blind will (Schopenhauer), or impulsion of life (Bergson), because that they "studied habitual Mind through introspection", i.e. they remained on irrational instincts and desires. Although Xiong Shili did not deny Bergson's philosophy of life, he did not approve of Bergson's view to put impulsion of life and reason in opposition. In his view, Will should come from self-consciousness, that is, it should be based on the rational knowledge. Therefore, Xiong Shili repeatedly stressed "the advocacy of anti-reason and the abandonment of speculation displayed all the extremes." (*Important Quotations from Xiong Shili*, vol.3) Although his view was not new in theory, its theoretic significance could not be neglected in correcting the prejudice of the modern voluntarist tendency. In contrast with Liang Shuming's elaboration on the theory of "Idea is the dominator of Mind" of Wang Yangming's philosophy of the Taizhou Sect, Xiong Shili's view on the relation between will and reason seems closer to the original philosophy of Wang Yangming.

Disagreeing with Xiong Shili's elaboration of Wang Yangming's theory of attainment of innate knowledge mainly on the relation between Nature (transcendental Nature) and cultivation (moral cultivation), He Lin[1] concentrated on Wang Yangming's theory of the unity of knowledge and action. He put forth the new theory of the unity of knowledge and action, and its substance was obviously influenced by Wang Yangming's theory of knowledge and action.

He Lin held that knowledge and action could be divided into different degrees respectively, and knowledge was unfolded as a course from a lower state to a higher state. Undoubtedly, this view has some similarity to Wang Yangming's distinction between original knowledge and apperceptive knowledge. As a matter of fact, He Lin also noticed this connection, and said: "Yangming also thought there was difference of degrees." (*New Theory of Unity of Knowledge and Action*) In Wang Yangming's theory, the distinction between original knowledge and apperceptive knowledge constituted the prerequisite of the unity between knowledge and action: The double transformation from natural knowledge to apperceptive knowledge was realized through action. This logical relation was also reflected in He Lin's new theory of the unity of knowledge and action. Starting from the view that there existed degrees of knowledge and action respectively, He Lin held that a certain degree of knowledge was always correspondent to a certain degree of action, and the unity of knowledge and action was unfolded at different degrees. However, in comparison with Wang Yangming's idea of connecting the unity of knowledge and action with the return to the transcendental innate knowledge, He Lin's understanding

---

[1] He Lin (1902 – 1992), a philosopher, historian, and educator, one of the leading figures of modern Neo-Confucianism. He was the first to translate many Western philosophical works into Chinese.

of unity of knowledge and action seemed to embody a concept of development to a great extent.

In He Lin's view, this unity of knowledge and action could be studied from the dual aspects of the individual and the community. As far as the individual is concerned, anyone's knowledge and action were unified; He Lin specially emphasized the guiding function of knowledge over action, and held that conduct without knowledge was either wanton action, blind action, or passive action, and inevitably valueless. (*Discussion and Elaboration of the Relation between Knowledge and Action*) This view certainly reflects the standpoint of rationalism.

In connection with the individual's unity of knowledge and action was the community's unity of knowledge and action: "The theory of the community's unity of knowledge and action refers to the unity of knowledge and action in consideration of great causes run by a group or a community." "Again as far as the standards and levels of knowledge of of a given time or society are concerned, they are always in harmony and conformity." (*Ibid.*) Here, knowledge and action have exceeded the scope of the individual's cultivation of Mind and Nature, and been unfolded as the community's great cause. This view doubtlessly has a greater vision than that of Wang Yangming. An even more noteworthy point is that He Lin affirmed that different times had different levels of knowledge and action, which in a sense already touched the historicity of the unity of knowledge and action. He Lin's view not only inherited the theory of the course of the attainment of innate knowledge from Wang Yangming to Huang Zongxi, but also further promoted the theory of the unity of knowledge and action through the absorption of the concept of evolution.

It can be seen that from the late Ming Dynasty to the modern times, Wang Yangming's Mindology experienced a long historical evolution, and exerted multi-faceted influences on the intellectual and cultural domains. In a sense, if we ignore Wang Yangming's Mindology, we will find it difficult to understand the Chinese intellectual and cultural history after the middle Ming Dynasty as a whole.

Appendices

I. Bibliography

Chen Xianzhang, *The Complete Works of Baishazi* 陈献章《白沙子全集》

Cheng Hao & Cheng Yi, *The Posthumous Writings of Two Chengs* 程颢、程颐《二程遗书》

He Lin, *New Theory of the Unity of Knowledge and Action* 贺麟《知行合一新论》

Huang Zongxi, *Academic Cases of Confucian Scholars in the Ming Dynasty* 黄宗羲《明儒学案》;

    Academic Cases of the Confucian Scholars in the Song and Yuan Dynasties 《宋元学案》;

    Five Collections of Mr. Nanlei Wending 《南雷文定五集》;

    On Master Meng Zi 《孟子师说》;

    Records in Waiting for a Visit in Darkness 《明夷待访录》

Kang Youwei, *Elucidation on Meng Zi* 康有为《孟子微》

Li Zhi, *Collected Works of Li Wenling* 李贽《李温陵集》;

    On the Burning of Books 《焚书》

Liang Qichao, *Confucian Philosophy* 梁启超《儒家哲学》;

    On the New People 《新民说》

Liang Shumin, *Gists of the Chinese Culture* 梁漱溟《中国文化要义》;

    The East and West Cultures and Their Philosophies 《东西文化及其哲学》

Liu Zongzhou, *Complete Collection of Liuzi* 刘宗周《刘子全书》

Lu Jiuyuan, *Collected Writings of Lu Jiuyuan* 陆九渊《陆九渊集》

Luo Hongxian, *Collected Writings of Mr. Luo Nian'an* 罗洪先《念庵罗先生文集》

Luo Rufang, *Important Quotations of Mr. Luo Jinxi* 罗汝芳《罗近溪先生语要》

Ouyang De, *Collected Writings of Mr. Ouyang Nanye* 欧阳德《欧阳南野先生文集》

Tan Sitong, *Complete Collection of Tan Sitong* 谭嗣同《谭嗣同全集》

Tang Zhen, *The Book of Retreat* 唐甄《潜书》

Wang Dong, *Posthumous Collection of Mr. Wang Yi'an* 王栋《王一庵先生遗集》

Wang Gen, *Posthumous Collection of Mr. Wang Xinzhai* 王艮《王心斋先生遗集》

Wang Ji, *Complete Collection of Mr. Wang Longxi* 王畿《王龙溪先生全集》

Wang Shouren, *Records of the Instructions and Reviews* 王守仁《传习录》;
  The Complete Collection of Yangming 《阳明全书》;
  The Complete Works of Wang Yangming 《王阳明全集》

Xiong Shili, *Important Quotations from Xiong Shili* 熊十力《十力语要》

Xu Heng, *Posthumous Writings of Luzhai* 许衡《鲁斋遗书》

Yang Jian, *Posthumous Writings of Cihu* 杨简《慈湖遗书》

Zhou Dunyi, *The Exposition of the Ultimate Diagram* 周敦颐《太极图说》

Zhu Xi, *Categorized Quotations from Zhu Xi* 朱熹《朱子语类》;
  Collected Writings of Master Zhu 《朱文公文集》;
  Questions on Meng Zi 《孟子或问》;
  Questions on the Four Books 《四书或问》

Zou Shouyi, *Collected Writings of Mr. Zou Dongkuo* 邹守益《东廓邹先生文集》

Commentary on the Sutra of Perfect Enlightenment 《圆觉经大疏钞》
The Zhou Book of Change 《周易》

II. Glossary

apperceptive knowledge 明觉之知 (míng jué zhī zhī) 77, 78, 82, 113, 154

aspiration/determination 立志 (lì zhì) 17, 43, 54, 63, 64, 73, 93, 95, 96, 97, 102

benevolence 仁 (rén) 11, 16, 32, 60, 69, 70, 71, 86, 93, 128, 129

benevolent Principle 仁道原则 (rén dào yuán zé) 32

Child-Mind 童心 (tóng xīn) 90, 100, 101, 102, 104, 105, 107, 109, 110, 132

Confucianism 儒学 (rú xué) 2, 3, 62, 65, 73, 75, 79, 91, 99, 140, 143, 151

cosmology 宇宙论 (yǔ zhòu lùn) 12, 39, 43, 46

course of attainment of innate knowledge 致知过程 (zhì zhī guò chéng) 112, 116, 153

distinction between Heaven and Man 天人之辨 (tiān rén zhī biàn) 30, 94

distinction between Mind and Nature 心性之辨 (xīn xìng zhī biàn) 16, 28, 29, 91, 133

distinction between Mind and Thing 心物之辨 (xīn wù zhī biàn) 28, 38, 44

distinction between the self and the community 群己之辨 (qún jǐ zhī biàn) 61, 62, 69, 72, 73, 74, 75, 134, 135

Donglin Sect 东林学派 (dōng lín xué pài) 112, 121, 122

Effort Sect 工夫派 (gōng fū pài) 117, 118, 119, 120, 121, 122, 127

essentialism 本质主义 (běn zhì zhǔ yì) 12, 34, 107, 109, 110

evaluation of value 价值评价 (jià zhí píng jià) 53, 96, 97

existence 存在 (cún zài) 8, 9, 11, 12, 13, 14, 15, 17, 19, 20, 23, 29, 31, 33, 34, 35, 37, 38, 39, 40, 41, 42, 43, 44, 45, 46, 50, 51, 52, 53, 58, 60, 61, 62, 65, 66, 67, 68, 70, 71, 75, 76, 80, 81, 85, 89, 92, 93, 95, 100, 102,